A River Apart

ROBERT SUTHERLAND

Fitzhenry & Whiteside

A River Apart

ISBN 1-55041-652-9

Fitzhenry & Whiteside acknowledges with thanks the Canada Council for the Arts, the Government of Canada through its Book Publishing Industry Development Program, and the Ontario Arts Council for their support in our publishing program.

10 9 8 7 6 5 4 3 2

Canadian Cataloguing in Publication Data

Sutherland, Robert, 1925-
  A river apart

ISBN 1-55041-652-9 (bound)   ISBN 1-55041-646-4 (pbk.)

1.Canada – History – War of 1812 – Juvenile fiction.* 2. United States – History – War of 1812 – Juvenile fiction. I. Title.

PS8587.U798R58 2000   jC813'.54   C00-932055-5
PZ7.S96692Ri 2000

Design: Darrell McCalla
Cover illustration: Brian Deines

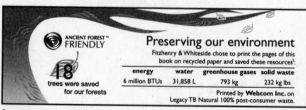

ANCIENT FOREST™ FRIENDLY

Preserving our environment
Fitzhenry & Whiteside chose to print the pages of this book on recycled paper and saved these resources[1]:

energy	water	greenhouse gases	solid waste
6 million BTUs	31,858 L	793 kg	232 kg lbs

18 trees were saved for our forests

Printed by Webcom Inc. on Legacy TB Natural 100% post-consumer waste.

[1]Estimates were made using the Environmental Defense Paper Calculator.

FSC

Mixed Sources
Product group from well-managed forests, controlled sources and recycled wood or fiber

Cert no. SW-COC-002358
www.fsc.org
© 1996 Forest Stewardship Council

For Monica, Fiona
and Lachlan
And in fond memory
of Allan
With love

A River Apart

The War of 1812

Angered by British interference with
their ships in neutral waters during the
Napoleonic wars, the Americans declared war
on Britain on June 18, 1812,
hoping to annex British North America (Canada)
to the republic. This story is based on
the following events that
took place during the War of 1812-14.

July 22, 1812 – The plan to capture the British gunboat in Prescott, abandoned because of the American Militia's refusal to cross the river.

October 3, 1812 – The failed attempt by the British/Canadian forces to capture the American guns at Ogdensburg.

February 22, 1813 – The successful capture of the guns at Ogdensburg, when the British/Canadian forces crossed the river on the ice, which resulted in the return to almost normal relations between the people of Ogdensburg, New York and Prescott, Ontario.

October 25, 1813 – The battle of Chateauguay.

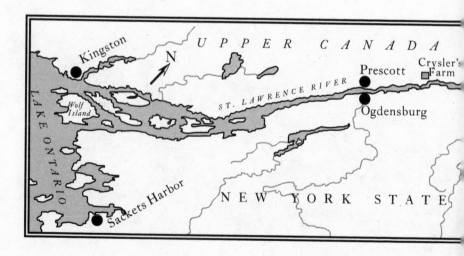

November 11, 1813 – General Wilkinson's drive down the St. Lawrence River toward Montreal, ending in the Battle of Crysler's Farm.

The following historical people appear in or are mentioned in the story:

British/Canadians: Major-General Isaac Brock; Lieutenant-Colonel "Red George" Macdonell; Lieutenant-Colonel Joseph Morrison.

Americans: President James Madison; Henry Clay, Speaker of the House; Major-General Wade Hampton; Commodore Oliver Hazard Perry; Lieutenant-Colonel Solomon Van Rensselaer; General Stephen Van Rensselaer; Major General James Wilkinson.

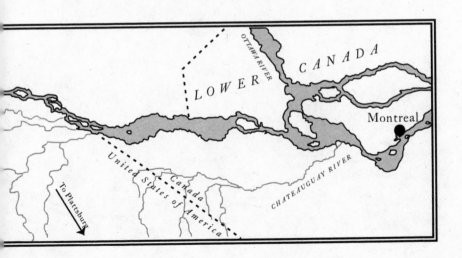

Chapter One

There was something wrong. James sensed it as soon as he left his beached canoe and turned toward the house.

At first there wasn't anything obvious to explain the feeling of dread. The Jacksons' fine frame house stood behind the white picket fence, the trees of the orchard visible beyond. A plume of smoke from the chimney indicated life as usual within. Everything *seemed* normal.

Ordinarily now, he would approach the house, whistling cheerily. Jared and Leah would come to meet him, but Pilot would arrive first, tail wagging furiously, barking a welcome. James would rub the dog's ears and tickle his tummy, and then his two friends would conduct him into the big, warm kitchen. There Mrs. Jackson, plump and motherly, would easily persuade him to stow away several of her light, fluffy pancakes, smothered in maple syrup. Even arrogant Mr. Jackson might look in, nodding his lean face in a formal acknowledgment of James' presence. So what was different about today? Nothing, surely.

He puckered his lips to begin his approach. He would have to whistle a little louder this morning to be heard above that noise...he stopped. That noise! It had been there all the time, a background noise that just now registered on his ear. It wasn't very loud, but it shouldn't have been there at all.

It came from the barn across the road from the Jacksons'. The cattle! They were lowing. Not just an occasional moo, but a steady complaint, as if they were uncomfortable and were trying to attract attention.

They should have been milked by now, but evidently had not been. Something *was* up. Something had disturbed his neighbor's routine, at least.

Curious, James started toward the sound, but something else attracted his attention. As he passed the end of the Jacksons' house, he saw two buggies and a number of horses – at least eight in all – tethered to the veranda rail.

What had happened? He was aware of a growing uneasiness. Something had happened to the Jacksons. Perhaps Mr. Jackson had had a heart attack. That would bring a crowd of sympathizers to the door, for he was a prominent lawyer and legislator. James hesitated. What should he do? Should he go to the door and enquire, or would he be intruding? Perhaps he should slip away, back home across the St. Lawrence River, before his presence was detected.

His mind was made up for him. The back door of the Jacksons' home opened. There was no sign of either Pilot or Jared. Only Leah appeared. She stood for a moment on the stoop, undecided. Then she hitched up her long skirts and was running toward him, her black hair flying. And when she came near, he saw that her face was white and there were tears in her dark eyes.

"What is it?" he asked. "There's something wrong. Is it your father?"

"Oh no. No." She bit her lip. "No, it's…Jamie, you can't come here any more."

"I can't come here!" He stared at her, bewildered. "Why? What do you mean? Why can't I…?"

She made an impatient gesture. "It's…it's stupid. It's horrible. But you can't come. Father won't let us have anything more to do with you. Haven't you heard, Jamie? We're at war!"

"At war! Who's at war? Oh!" Comprehension dawned. There had been talk of war, of course, in that fateful year of 1812 – of the republic to the south threatening to make war on that part of North America – the Canadas – still occupied by the British; something to do with revenge for high handed actions by the Royal Navy in enforcing the blockade of Napoleonic France. American ships had been prevented from trading with Britain's enemy. And there was the desire of some angry Americans to add British North America to their republic. But surely it had been nothing more than talk – talk by a few hot-headed 'war hawks'.

"Has it really come to this?" He could scarcely believe it. But she nodded dumbly. "But, even so, it's got nothing to do with us, has it?" He spoke desperately. "We're friends. We're neighbors."

She wouldn't look him in the eye. "Not any more. We're enemies. Father says so." She pointed to the river. "That's the dividing line. Anyone living over there is our enemy. Until this war is over. Then we can be friends again." She spoke tonelessly as if she had memorized the words.

James shook his head. "I can't believe it. Why should friends fight friends? You're not *my* enemy, Leah. Nor is Jared, or your mother. *Or* your father. This war won't touch us, Leah. Let armies fight it out if they have to." He knew he was trying to convince himself as well as her. "Don't you believe that?"

She looked up at him then. There were tears in her eyes. "We're friends. We always will be. But for now, we're at war. We're enemies. Father says it won't be long. Britain is fighting France and won't be able to defend your country too. We will soon liberate you and make you a part of us. Then it will be all over and we can be friends again."

"Liberate us? From what? Leah, we don't need to be liberated from anything. My family was driven off our land in Virginia because we remained loyal to Britain. Now we have our own land there across the river, and we're happy the way we are. If we want a change, we'll get it ourselves. Our people won't be forced into joining you or anyone else. If I have to, I'll join in. We'll fight for what we have."

"Oh no. Not you, Jamie. Please, not you. Why do men want war! It's horrible. There's a captain of militia in the house there now, meeting with father, calling for recruits. And father's backing him up. Even Jared…." She faltered.

"Jared? What about him?"

"He – he's excited. Of course he's only fourteen, but the captain says he could be a drummer and help in recruiting. But that would mean he would leave home, even if he never fights. And father is encouraging him. And Jamie…?" she suddenly caught his hand in hers, her cool fingers clutching his, "*you* won't really have to…will you?"

"I don't know. It may all blow over very soon. And it may not touch us at all." He hesitated. The door had opened again. Jared Jackson stood there, his hand still on the latch, when a small black form shot between his legs and bounded across the yard barking a welcome.

"Pilot! Come back!" But the dog paid no attention. He thrust himself between Leah and James, reaching up, tail wagging.

"Good boy. *We're* still friends, aren't we, Pilot." James knelt and rubbed the dog's ears, then looked up. Jared was striding toward them, his usually friendly face blank.

"Pilot! Come here!"

The dog looked from one to the other, as if puzzled.

James faced his friend. "Jared," he said carefully, "Leah has been telling me. I can hardly believe it."

A stern look was struggling to replace the natural friendliness on Jared's freckled face.

"It's true. We're at war, James. You're not welcome here any more." He looked uncomfortable. "Father says so."

"I see." James tried to speak coldly, but it didn't work. Jared was only one year younger than both James and Leah, and they were best friends. "Leah says you want to go. To the army."

"Yes!" His face lit up. "It will be fun to march, and play a drum, and wear a uniform. And I'll probably never have to fight. I'll be attached to the garrison right here in Ogdensburg. President Madison says it's just a matter of marching before we win…" The sound came to them of the front door opening around the other side of the house. Jared looked apprehensive. "Come, Leah. Father won't like us talking to the enemy."

"Father doesn't need to know. Enemy or not, Jamie is our friend. You'd better go. He will be looking for you."

"Yes. Don't be long, Leah." He looked at James, his face a conflict of emotions. For a moment it seemed he was about to offer his hand in friendship, but he appeared to change his mind. "Bye, James." Then he was gone.

Leah looked at James, hurt in her eyes. "We are still friends, Jamie. No matter what. Will you still come to see me?"

He didn't hesitate over that. "Yes! As long as I can. I will want to know what's happening to Jared. He's still my friend. I love him. And you." He didn't look at her. He knew his face was burning. "I love you all like family. But…" He frowned. "I guess I won't be welcome in your house any longer. We would have to meet secretly, and I wouldn't want to do it that way. Your father…"

She sighed. "He needn't know. It will be just to let us each know what is going on – with you. And Jared. And me. I'll look out for you every Friday morning at this time, as always. If you don't show up, I'll know it's because you can't. And if you do come but I don't come to meet you, you will know it's because *I* can't. Not because I don't want to, or because we're enemies. In that case, just turn around and go home." There was pleading in her eyes. "Is that all right, Jamie?"

"Yes. Every Friday. Whenever I can. I don't know how this war will affect me. I hope, not at all. I'm a farmer, not a soldier. But…" He shrugged. He caught her hand and held it, tightly, for a long moment. Then he turned and launched his canoe and began to paddle over the river.

The river! An hour ago it had been a friend, smiling in the sun, linking nations and families. Now it was cold and gray and forbidding, a barrier, separating him from his friends. From Leah.

Why? It made no sense.

He shivered….

Chapter Two

Three weeks passed, and if their country was at war, no word of it reached the Shaws' farm. It had been a late spring and James and his father, Thomas Shaw, were too busy ploughing and planting to take the time to walk the few miles to the village of Prescott. Had they done so, activity around the newly built and not yet completed Fort Wellington would have told them that something unusual was in the air. As it was, nothing disturbed their spring schedule, working the fields from dawn to dusk, while Rachel Shaw and little Mary milked the cows, fed the chickens, baked and sewed, and swept the little log house that was their pride.

Not that the thought of war was entirely absent. It was there, like a cloud threatening to obscure the sunlight – an uncertain menace. And on the past three Fridays, James' thoughts turned even more than usual to the Jacksons across the river. And to Leah in particular. If there had been a deluge or a hard frost, or if something else had happened to hinder their work in the fields, he would have slipped his canoe into the river and, with his father's blessing, and aided by the current, have ventured once more to that house on the eastern outskirts of Ogdensburg. But the weather continued fine and they had to make the most of it.

He could only wonder, as he guided the plough behind the plodding oxen, if Leah had watched for him. Or had the opportunity to do so been denied her?

As he bent to remove a stone turned up by the plough, James thought of those parting words when he had left, and his cheeks burned when he remembered that he had said he loved her. Of course he had said he loved Jared too, and to soften the implication, he had included her entire family. Brotherly love. Did she know it was more than that? Had she even noticed? He almost hoped she hadn't. It could complicate their friendship.

Perhaps she had resented it. But no, she was the one who had planned their future meeting. He kicked a clod of earth resentfully out of the way. This stupid war!

But perhaps it had all blown over, or surely some word would have reached them by now.

Apparently his father had been reading James' mind. When they reached the end of a furrow, Thomas clapped his son on the back.

"You'll see, lad," he said confidently. "Cooler heads will prevail. No one on this side of the river and few on the other side want to spill blood. It will all blow over and you can go back to see your friends anytime. All this talk of war will be forgotten."

But it was not to be.

That afternoon an army officer, decked out in his red coat, rode up to the farm. Father and son watched him coming, and they knew they had been wrong. "Now we'll know," murmured Thomas Shaw, and went to meet the rider.

They spoke a few words, then the officer dismounted. Mr. Shaw beckoned his son and they went together into the small, warm kitchen.

Rachel was there, her arms white with flour to the elbow, and little Mary looked up from her place in front of the fire. Rachel's face paled with apprehension.

"My dear," said Thomas gently, "this is Captain MacKessock of the Grenville militia. He has come to have a word with us. This is my wife, sir. Mrs. Shaw."

James' mother inclined her head in answer to the officer's bow. "Please," she said, "be seated." Then, when he had done so, "Is it to be war, then?"

"Yes ma'am, I'm afraid so. The Yankees are determined to invade us. And we are determined to defend ourselves."

"So…?" She looked away, for a moment, to the window through which she could see their land sloping down to the river. Then she caught little Mary up in her arms and turned, her eyes challenging those of the officer. "Have you come to take our men away from us?"

"No, ma'am. At least not yet. I just want everyone to know the situation. I am calling upon all the farms in the area to let you know. Most of the people are, like yourselves, Tories who left their homes in Virginia,

Pennsylvania, or New York, to remain loyal to the British flag. And some of you suffered for your loyalty."

Thomas Shaw nodded briefly. "Our home was burned. We lost everything."

"So there's no question of your loyalty. Now," he turned to Rachel, "as to your question. The Glengarry Light Infantry is stationed at Prescott where, as you know, we are in the process of building a fort. They are, of course, regulars, and will have to go wherever we are needed. And you must know we are badly outnumbered in every sphere. They may be called out to repulse the enemy anywhere from Detroit to Montreal. If anyone volunteers to join us, he will be welcomed, but we are not putting pressure on anyone to do so. What we do need is some part-time soldiers to call on for emergencies. Militia."

Thomas reached out his hand to hold Rachel's. "What would you call an emergency, Captain?"

In answer the officer turned and pointed out the window to the river. "That river, sir, and the road behind us, are the only supply routes between Upper and Lower Canada. Any supplies and reinforcements coming from Britain and bound for Kingston and beyond must use one of those routes. And certainly the river will be first choice. The road right now is axle deep in mud in many places.

"Sooner or later the Yankees are going to try to cut that supply route. And the obvious place to do so is along here, where the river is no more than a mile wide."

Mr. Shaw rubbed his stubbly jaw thoughtfully. "It seems to me that, as long as we hold the fort, we can control the river. Unless they have the same or better in Ogdensburg –"

"Maybe they have," broke in James. "Certainly there is a garrison there."

Captain McKessock turned to him. "Now how would you know that?"

James flushed at suddenly being addressed by the officer. "I was visiting the Jacksons – they're my friends – soon after war was declared. That's where I first heard about it. My friend Jared said he was going to be a drummer and would be stationed at the Ogdensbug garrison. That's all. I don't know anything else about it."

"Jared Jackson? Would that be Malachi Jackson's boy?" At James' nod the captain smiled briefly. "You will not be welcomed there any more, will you. Malachi Jackson is one of the few people in Ogdensburg who is hot for war. He's frustrated these days. Our people and theirs are still trading and visiting across the river as if nothing is happening. He's trying to put a stop to that, without much success. But yes, there is a garrison there, which they're building up and adding guns to match ours. They will play havoc with shipping on the river. Sooner or later we are going to have to go over there and silence those guns. An open river is vital."

To go across. And silence the guns. And Jared would be there, defending those guns. Jared, his friend, Leah's brother – enemies!

James scarcely heard the captain continuing.

"We are asking for volunteers to take training at the fort whenever possible. Not to go to Detroit, or York, or Niagara, or Kingston, but to defend our own land and keep the river open. I do not require an answer today, but I want you to think it over –"

"Just a minute." Thomas Shaw stood up. He put his arm around his wife and faced the officer. "As I said, we lost everything once. I will not let that happen again. I will do as you ask. I cannot answer for the boy. He is barely fifteen and has good friends on the other side. It is up to him. I will respect his decision."

Captain MacKessock turned to James. "So will I. There is no need to answer now, lad. Mr. Shaw, there will be a first training session at the Fort come Tuesday. As early as you can make it." He stood up and bowed to Rachel. "Your servant, ma'am. I am sorry to be the bearer of bad news, but…" He shrugged and turned. "I will be on my way."

He had reached the door when James spoke. "Wait," he said.

James thought of the land he had been ploughing a few minutes earlier. Beyond that were stumps of trees laboriously cut down, the stumps still to be removed or burned. Hours of toil and sweat had gone into tilling the soil and building the house. But it was *their* land. He knew what it was like, from his father's tales, to have land taken away by force – to have nothing left. It mustn't happen again. Even if it meant the unthinkable: face Jared from behind the barrel of a musket. Decide in a split second. Lose Jared. And Leah. Forever. Or his own life. No! Please God that would never happen.

James closed his mind to all that, shutting it out. He saw an invading army, the house in flames, his mother and sister brutalized, and he knew what his answer had to be.

"I will come too," he said.

And he would have to see Leah, once more, before this stupid war changed their lives forever.

Chapter Three

Major Wilson of the United States Army dismounted and hitched his horse to the railing of the Jacksons' veranda. The door was opened by a girl in the bloom of young womanhood, with black hair, dark eyes and rose-tinted cheeks.

"Welcome, sir," she said. "Father is waiting for you in the parlor."

The major bowed. "Thank you. To whom do I have the pleasure of speaking?"

"I am Leah, sir. Leah Jackson."

"Ah. Jared's sister. Your brother is becoming a very competent drummer." He looked at her with obvious admiration. "Your father has reason to be proud of his family."

She opened her lips to reply, then thought better of it.

"If you will come this way, sir. Tea will be served. Or coffee, if you prefer."

* * *

"It must stop." Malachi Jackson leaned forward, his fingers rapping on the table for emphasis. "Major Wilson, you must put a stop to it."

"Oh, I don't know." The tea service had been removed by a maid in a crisp white uniform, and the two men were alone in the parlor, facing each other. Neither noticed that the door behind Mr. Jackson was ajar. "I think you're reacting too strongly, sir. People who have been friendly for years and have visited back and forth are going to resent any interference. Besides, our Canadian friends bring us important information. For instance, a detachment of the Glengarries has been ordered west to the Detroit sector. We have dispatched a scout to General Hull with that news. It also means that the Fort at Prescott is now manned by militia, along with a skeleton command of regulars, of course. That is valuable information, sir."

"Oh, no doubt. But I'm sure it works both ways. Our people will be betraying our position too. Not intentionally, of course, but damaging for all that."

"No, sir, we don't have to worry about that. Simply because our people don't *know* anything that would be of value to the enemy. The number and position of our guns? They already have that information. We've made no effort to disguise it. I don't know anything that would help them, so I'm sure no one else does."

Malachi Jackson wasn't convinced. "You must have some information you share with your officers. The High Command's strategy, for instance…"

"Well, yes." The major was amused. "We're attacking on three fronts. Across the rivers at Detroit and Niagara, and sending a force up from Plattsburg to take Montreal. All of which are well known to the enemy, I assure you."

"But, why not here, where the river is at its narrowest?"

Major Wilson made an impatient gesture. "I'm sure the High Command has its reasons. Think about it, sir. Three attacks from points as far separated as Detroit and Montreal. Why, that's five hundred miles or more. They will have to spread their forces very thinly indeed. And their forces are very thin to begin with."

Malachi Jackson nodded, doubtfully. "We have superiority on every front, I presume?"

"Numerical superiority, undoubtedly. But that doesn't necessarily guarantee success in a war such as this."

"What do you mean, a war such as this?"

"You must admit, sir, it's an unpopular war. And they have a very competent commander in General Brock. *And* they're defending their homeland. I know, we tell ourselves we're liberating them, and they'll welcome us with open arms." Major Wilson shook his head. "That, sir, is simply not true. Oh, there are some…a few who left our country because land was cheap over there. They might welcome us. But the majority will oppose us to the death. And then there's our militia."

"What about our militia?"

"Like the Canadians, they would defend their homeland to the last. That's what they're recruited for. But leaving their own country to invade another…that's a different matter. Their hearts won't be in it."

"That's exactly what I'm talking about, Major," broke in Mr. Jackson eagerly. "That's the problem here in Ogdensburg, except we're talking about civilians. How can the hearts of the people be in it when they're allowed to visit back and forth with the enemy? If we're going to win this war we're going to have to change the attitude of the people, and we can begin right here."

"How do you suggest we do that?"

"By closing the river, of course. Forbidding our people to cross over. Arresting any of theirs who come here, and charging them with spying. Turn our people against them. Harsh measures, sir. It's up to you and your command to enforce it. Your job is to close the river, is it not?"

"Yes sir. To supplies, troop movements, reinforce-ments…"

"Then do so. *Any* enemy movements. That includes civilians who for all we know may be spies. Open fire on them before they land – even rowboats or canoes. That will soon change their minds and convince our people that we are really at war, and they are enemies. Enemies, sir!"

"We can do that, of course. If that is the direction from your council. We are ordered to cooperate with the town. I understand you can speak for the council?"

"You understand correctly. We have a few on council who are lacking in patriotic fervor, but I have made my will known and have swayed them to my way of thinking.

Do we understand each other then? *Any* of their people who land in our town – or neighborhood – will be imprisoned awaiting trial for espionage. Have I made our position clear?"

"Perfectly, sir."

"Very well, then. I am pleased we have had this conversation. Now, sir, would you like a glass of port before you are on your way?"

When Major Wilson left, it was the young girl again who showed him to the door. He noticed fleetingly that her face had paled, accentuating the darkness of her eyes in an ashen face. He wondered vaguely what had disturbed her.

Chapter Four

It was still dark, with only the faintest hint of the coming dawn in the eastern sky, when Leah slipped out the back door, easing it gently closed again so as to make no sound.

Pilot stirred at his place on the stoop, opening one sleepy eye enquiringly.

"Hush, Pilot. Go back to sleep." She gave him a quick pat on the head. "Don't make a sound. Don't give me away."

She pulled the black hood over her head, hesitated a moment, peering into the darkness, then ran down the path through the trees. She needed no light for this part of the journey. She knew every inch of the beloved orchard. But she had to stop, hitch up her cloak and the long night-dress underneath, to clamber awkwardly over the snake rail fence that separated the orchard from the pasture. She knew then, by sound rather than sight, that there were cattle nearby, moving heavily away from her. And she knew there were patches of their dung, darker blotches on a black field, that she had to try to avoid if possible. Where the grass was long, the dew soaked through her shoes – little more than slippers – and soaked the hem of her cloak. She barely noticed. She reached the edge of the field and was faced by another rail fence. She climbed over, catching her night-dress on the top rail, wrenching it free, leaving a piece of it behind...

She was in the village now. The scattered houses were in darkness, except for one where a candle burned in a window. Once a dog barked a deep, menacing bark. She caught her breath in fear. But an angry voice in an unseen bedroom told the dog to shut up, and it obeyed. She crossed a lane that led to the river where the dancing light of a fire reflected off the black barrel of one of the guns pointing across the river at the 'enemy.' That would be the fire kept going all night to heat the water for the sentries' tea. Pretty soon those sentries would be waking Jared so that he, in turn, could waken the garrison with his morning drum roll. Jared – what would he do if he knew what she was doing, where she was going?

She shut that thought from her mind. Her only concern must be for Jamie. If he was coming – and pray God he wasn't – then this would be the day. It was a Friday morning. In another week, the news of the forceful closing of the river would surely have reached the other side, but today Jamie would have no idea of the violent welcome awaiting him. She knew his routine. He would cross the river opposite his home and paddle along the American shore. And that would take him right in front of the guns that now were ordered to blast anyone from the Canadian side out of the water.

Her only hope was to stop Jamie before he reached the village. She knew he would start out before daylight – and in these long summer days, that would be early indeed. So she too had started out in the small hours, pulling a long black cloak over her night-dress. Thank heavens her father had left the previous morning for Washington. She wasn't even sure how she was going to explain all this to her mother, if she was unable to creep back to her bed without being seen. But there was no time to worry about that.

Beyond the village, it was all unknown territory. Soon she was scrambling over hillocks, down sudden ravines, splashing through a stream, and pushing through clutching bushes – all the time casting anxious glances over her shoulder, until the last flicker of light from the sentries' fire was hidden by a hill on a point of land that reached out into the river.

She scrambled down to the bank once more, staring into the darkness. Light was reaching into the eastern sky but it was still dark down here. Jamie could be close without her realizing it. She listened, aching to hear the sound of a paddle dipping into the water, half hoping, half fearing that he was coming. But she heard only the frogs and crickets in chorus. Jamie would have no idea she was there and might easily slip by before she could attract his attention.

But she had come prepared. A fire on the shore would surely catch his eye, and he would come close to investigate – wouldn't he? She was counting on it. The trouble was, it might attract unwanted attention. But that was a chance she would have to take.

She reached into the deep pockets of her cloak and pulled out a tinderbox. Then she felt around for a flat, dry place on which to light a fire. She found a rock and spread the tinder on it – dry cotton cloth and powdered bark that would surely catch when she produced a spark. But she would need more than that to keep a fire going. Again she felt around, smothering her growing impatience with some effort. Everything was wet with dew. It would never catch. But wait. Perhaps underneath…yes. Under the top layer there were dry twigs and a small branch that snapped easily into manageable lengths.

She slipped out of the cloak. She would be more easily seen in her pale white night-dress. She shivered as the cool morning air penetrated its thin fabric, but she couldn't even think about that. She knelt over the pile of tinder and with trembling fingers struck flint on steel. Once, twice, then a spark, another spark, licking at the twigs. She blew on it, gently, coaxing. Carefully she laid the branches across the flame and held her breath. They were catching! The fire was going. Surely it would attract Jamie's attention – if he was coming. Jamie's and no one else's.

A figure emerged from the shadows behind her – a figure made unnaturally tall and broad by shako and epaulettes. A figure that carried a musket. She had no idea it was there.

Jamie saw the fire.

He was paddling casually, savoring the cool morning air, alive with the possibility of seeing Leah again. And maybe Jared too. No, that was most unlikely. The boy would be caught up in his new duties and would be too aware of his father's wishes to distance himself from the enemy. But Leah? Had she been on the lookout for him on those Fridays that had passed since their last meeting? Would she be there today, or had she given up? He desperately hoped she had not, for this would have to be the last chance – the last meeting until the war was ended.

He saw the fire. First a spark, then a growing flame. Some obscure movement beside the flames. Then suddenly there was a phantom there, a ghost, pale in the flickering light. His heart thudded in alarm at the strange apparition. He almost dropped his paddle from suddenly nerveless fingers, and the drifting canoe bumped the bank.

"Jamie! Thank God!"

He stared. It couldn't be…

"Leah?" A whisper, wondering, amazed. Then, "*Leah! Is that you? What…*" And at that moment he saw the dark, menacing figure behind her. "Leah!" he cried.

He sprang up. The canoe tipped, dropping him into the water. He scrambled up the bank. "Leah! Look out. Behind you!" And he pushed her aside and launched himself at the unknown danger, realizing, with a shock, even as he pushed it aside, that a moment before a musket had been threatening his very life. James and the stranger fell to the ground, struggling until the stranger pushed himself back from James' clutching fingers and gasped breathlessly.

"James! James, it's me. Jared!"

James rolled clear and stared in bewilderment at the brother and sister.

"Jared!" said Leah, faintly. "Why...? What...?" She snatched up her cloak and wrapped it around her. "Jared!" she gasped with sudden fear at the sight of the musket at their feet. "What...you weren't going to..."

"I came to do the same thing you came to do, I guess. To warn James, to stop him somehow..."

"Oh, Jared!" She reached out suddenly and caught him in a glad embrace. "I thought you would disapprove."

"I *do* disapprove." He tried to push himself from her arms, embarrassed. "I should take you both prisoner – James for spying and you for aiding and abetting the enemy."

"Then you will have to arrest yourself for the same reason." She laughed a little hysterically. "How did you ever get away? I thought you were on duty."

"I told the captain I was sick. He told me to go home and take my gun with me so I could practice loading when I felt better. I need lots of practice to meet his standards –"

"What is this," broke in James, totally bewildered, "about a *spy?*"

"That's you. If you had come ashore at our house you would have been taken prisoner. That goes for anyone who comes over here from Canada from now on. But you wouldn't have gotten that far. Our guns have orders to fire on anyone – even canoes – that come onto our side of the river."

James' face had paled. "You saved my life," he said in wonder. "You risked your own safety. You *could* be arrested, both of you. I don't know how to thank you."

"I just did it for Leah," said Jared roughly. "She likes you for some reason. I had no idea she was doing the same thing till I saw the fire, and her standing there in her night-dress."

"I *had* to." She was glad the darkness hid her burning cheeks. "Jamie would never have seen me in that cloak."

"Forget it, Leah," James spoke softly. "He's joking. I'm very grateful to you both. But if what you say is true, this will be the last time I see you – either of you – until this war is over."

"Maybe not," said Jared, his voice tight. "I thought you would be in the army by now, James."

"No. I'm taking training, to be called on in an emergency. For instance, if you try to invade –"

"Then we *might* meet again" For a moment they faced each other, each realizing and dreading the possibility. Then, at the same moment, they reached out and clasped each other's hand in a brief, wordless farewell. Jared turned away.

Leah stood like a statue. Her cheeks were no longer burning. They were deathly pale.

For a moment she faced him. "Jamie," she whispered. He didn't say anything. For a moment their eyes met in a message they were too shy to put into words. Then he broke away, turned, launched his canoe into the river, and headed for home.

Chapter Five

For a long moment Malachi Jackson gazed through his telescope at the opposite shore. There was a grim smile on his face when he saw what the lifting of the morning mist revealed. He lowered the glass and turned to the man beside him.

"That, sir, would be a prize worth taking. Would you not agree?"

"Let me see." Lieutenant-Colonel Solomon Van Rensselaer, a member of a prominent New York family and aide to his cousin, the general of the same name, took the glass and focused it on the object that had attracted Mr. Jackson's attention. He saw a gunboat, one of the shallow draft river boats, the only naval vessel that could navigate the St. Lawrence River. There was a single six-pounder cannon on the forecastle.

"Yes, indeed. I commend you for your foresight, Malachi. With that in our possession, we could control the river. I wonder if Major Wilson is aware of its existence." He turned to a man who stood a respectful distance behind them. "Sergeant, tell Major Wilson I wish to speak to him. Yes," he repeated, turning a keen eye on Mr. Jackson, "you suggest we capture the boat. Now, sir, how would you go about it?"

"How would I – oh no, Colonel. You're the soldier. But," he hesitated, "since you ask…it would have to be at night, of course. Cross over with muffled oars. Take them by surprise. Secrecy would be the key. No word must leak out beforehand. I regret we still have people in our town who couldn't be counted on to hold their tongues."

"Secrecy, yes. Surprise would be vital, as you say." The colonel turned the glass onto the gunboat again, then swept the opposite shore in both directions.

"You wanted me, sir?" Major Wilson approached.

"Yes, Major. Look at this." He handed the telescope to the other officer. "I'm just passing through on my way to the Niagara frontier, so I have no authority here, and Mr. Jackson is a civilian so, of course, neither has he. But he suggests we capture it. What do you think?"

"Capture what, sir? Oh. A gunboat. Must have arrived overnight. We could certainly make good use of that."

"There's no doubt about that." The colonel watched the major critically. "The question is, how would you go about it?"

"I think the colonel would be better qualified to answer that, sir."

"No, no. No doubt I have more military experience, but this requires local knowledge which I don't have. What do you suggest?"

Major Wilson swept the opposite shore both up and down river then lowered the glass. "I have a detailed map of the river in the office. If you would care to come with me?"

"Good. Come along, Mr. Jackson. We could use your enthusiasm as well as your perception."

In a few moments they were leaning over a large map on a table.

"What I would suggest, sir, is this." Major Wilson traced his proposed route with a blunt finger. "In the dead of night – perhaps three a.m. – we take some men, perhaps up to one hundred, two or three miles up river, then cross over and land on the Canadian side. Then we approach Prescott through the forest from the rear. At a pre-set time, another force crosses the river by boat. No doubt it would be discovered before landfall, but that wouldn't matter. Indeed, so much the better. While they are drawing the enemy's attention the land force will fall on them – on the enemy – from the rear. I venture to say, sir, that the gunboat would be ours."

"Excellent. I heartily support such a plan. But to ensure success, we would require someone to lead the landing party who has intimate knowledge of the area. It would be difficult or impossible otherwise. Do we have such a person?"

"Yes!" Mr. Jackson spoke eagerly. "My son, Jared, who is a drummer boy, is very friendly with a boy who lives right..." he hesitated, then jabbed his finger on a spot on the map "...right there. The Shaws. Together they have explored the land for miles on both sides of the river. My boy could lead your men to Prescott in absolute secrecy. Of that I have no doubt whatever. Indeed, the Shaws' farm would be the ideal landing spot for such an excursion. It's cleared to the river's edge and not more than two miles from Prescott."

"Well!" The colonel was impressed. "But a drummer boy, you say. Just a lad." He turned a searching eye on Mr. Jackson. "And, as you say, secrecy is the key."

Malachi Jackson flushed at the implied criticism. "Sir, he is my son. You can count on him to hold his tongue."

"Good. Then, Major, I suggest we have the boy in."

* * *

"Jackson! You are wanted in the major's office. Immediately."

Jared stared at the sergeant. "I? Me? Why would he want to see me?"

The sergeant shrugged. "God knows. There's no accounting for officers' whims. All I know is you are to report to him at once. And it's not just the major. That colonel's there too."

"The colonel!" Jared gulped. "I don't..." But the sergeant wasn't listening. He was leading the way, assuming that he was being followed. He stopped at the door to the commanding officer's room. "Right. In you go. And don't forget to salute or I'll have your hide."

It was dark inside after the bright outdoors. Jared stumbled over the door sill, managed to pull himself upright, executed a salute that he desperately hoped was adequate, then saw in surprise that his father was there too. He gaped.

"Here, lad." The colonel himself came to his rescue, pushing a chair forward with his boot. "Have a seat. We need your expert advice."

"My ad..." Were they joking? "Yes, sir. I mean...yes, *sir.*"

"It's like this," said the major, ignoring Jared's confusion. "First, I must impress on you the need for absolute secrecy. Whatever you hear in this room must go no further on pain of court martial –"

"All right, Major," broke in Van Rensselaer, "no need to terrify the boy. He'll swear to secrecy. That is all we require. His father will be responsible for his actions. Perhaps, Mr. Jackson, you would care to explain how your boy can be of help."

"Yes, Colonel. Jared," he said eagerly, "you have a wonderful opportunity to help your country achieve an important object. In Prescott there's a gunboat moored to the wharf. We intend to steal it from under their noses. To do that we propose sending a landing party upstream – maybe two miles. This party would cross the river and attack Prescott from the rear while another force stages a frontal attack. The problem is that of course it would have to be at night. So we need someone familiar enough with the terrain over there to lead the party in secret, in silence, and in darkness. I told the colonel you could do that."

Jared's pulse quickened as he visualized the undertaking.

He hesitated only a moment, then nodded. "Yes, sir, I could do that."

"Good lad! You do your father proud. Now, where would *you* suggest we land our men? As I see it, we would need a clearing."

A clearing! Oh yes, Jared knew where there was a clearing. The blood drained from his face.

His father was looking at him expectantly. "A clearing, Jared," he prompted. "A farm, cleared to the water's edge. You know."

Jared clenched his hands in his lap. He closed his eyes.

"Yes, Jared." His father leaned forward. "The Shaws."

He swallowed, hard. "Of course," he managed. "The Shaws. But they would be sure to hear us and raise the alarm."

"That's to be expected," nodded the colonel. "So we will have to take steps to prevent that. They will have to be silenced."

"Silenced? You mean, taken prisoner?"

"I mean silenced, one way or another. We prefer not to shed blood unnecessarily, especially civilian blood. But this is *war*, lad. You will have to become accustomed to violence. Now. You have agreed to lead our expedition." It was a statement, not a question.

"Yes, sir," said Jared faintly.

* * *

How could he lead an expedition that would put his friend's life at risk? On the other hand, how could he refuse? He couldn't, of course. He was a soldier. He had to obey orders.

Jared was staring out the window, sick at heart. He didn't hear Leah approach. She touched his shoulder.

"Jared, what is it? What's troubling you?"

"Nothing." He shook free from Leah's hand. "Nothing, Leah."

"It's *not* nothing. It's something serious. You can tell me."

"No, I can't tell you." He spoke fiercely. "I can't tell anyone. I never should have joined the army."

"Oh, is that it? Are you afraid, Jared? That's nothing to be ashamed of, you know. I think everyone must be afraid when going into battle. Is that it? *Is* there a battle coming?"

"No! No, it's not that. I'm not afraid. It…it's worse and there's nothing I can do about it. And when it's over you…you will hate me."

"Jared! For goodness sake! I could never…"

But he turned away and left her.

Chapter Six

No drum roll or bugle blast awakened the men. They were roused by hands on shoulders and low, urgent voices in their ears. And at two o'clock in the morning four hundred confused and sleepy men stumbled out into a cloudy, moonless night. At first the only light was the night watchmen's flickering fire, and, away across the river, the enemy's counterpart.

They fell in on the parade square as N.C.O.'s, the non-commissioned officers, in frustrated whispers, tried to bring some order out of chaos. "What in tarnation is going on?" The question could be heard all over the square.

"Silence in the ranks! You will find out soon enough...."

Eventually Major Wilson enlightened them.

As their eyes became accustomed to the dark, they recognized their commanding officer, with the visiting Colonel and the militant civilian, Malachi Jackson.

"Men," said the major, in a controlled voice that reached to the farthest rank, "you have been training in the art of combat for many weeks now. I can promise you that at last you are going to have an opportunity to put the practice to work. You have been ordered to keep silent because sound travels far, especially over water. The last thing we want is to be heard by the people on the other side of the river. We're going over there, and we're going to take them by surprise. Lieutenant-Colonel Van Rensselaer is going to speak to you, because he has a vital interest in tonight's action. Colonel."

"Thank you, Major. Lads, listen to me. I am aide and cousin to General Van Rensselaer, who is in command of our forces in the Niagara area, and I am on my way to join him. In the near future we will be invading Canada across the Niagara river. We are naturally anxious that no reinforcements or supplies reach the enemy in the meantime. And any such assistance must pass along the river you see in front of you. The guns we have are not the full answer. They prevent large-scale movements on the river, and that's good. But some shipments still get through on shallow-draft bateaus sticking close to the far shore. Even that is too much. Every little bit getting through will make our task that much more difficult. Don't misunderstand me. We will win. But the shorter the conflict, the more lives of your countrymen that will be spared. Tonight we can solve that problem. At the wharf in Prescott, there is a gunboat with a six-pounder on deck. With that in our possession, nothing on the river will be out of range of our guns. And that is what we're going to do tonight – go over there and capture that gunboat right from under their noses.

"Now, to do that, we need one hundred and twenty volunteers – that's all – to reach our objective. Boats are ready to carry eighty of you two miles upriver. You will then cross over and land on Canadian soil. There's a young lad here who knows every step of the way, even in the darkness. He will lead you to Prescott, and at the signal, you will fall on the enemy from the rear. Meantime the remaining forty will be crossing the river right here. You cannot count on surprise. I doubt very much their sentries will be asleep. So you may draw some fire from their cannon. But it will not last long – only until your comrades attack from the forest. Your aim is not to conquer the enemy, or even to take over the fort they're building. It is simply to capture that gunboat, and, in the confusion, get away again. Major Wilson himself will lead the cross-river party and will be responsible for the actual acquisition of the gunboat. Captain Wells will lead the rest of you.

"Now, as I said, we only need one hundred and twenty of you to volunteer. I'm afraid the majority of you will be disappointed. Unfortunately more than that number will create too much confusion. But the first one hundred and twenty of you to step forward will have this chance to find glory and to strike a blow for your country. I am now inviting you to volunteer."

There was no rush, but some began to move. "That's it, men," encouraged Major Wilson. "Muster over there with Captain Wells. Let me know, Captain, when we have reached our limit."

They came forward, fifteen – perhaps twenty – at a time, hesitant, some obviously waiting for their friends to make the first move. Then ten came. Then five. And eventually, none at all.

"Come come, lads," There was an edge in the major's voice. "We haven't reached our quota yet. How many, Captain?"

"Fifty, sir. Perhaps fifty-five. No more than sixty."

"Sixty? That's half our complement already." The major's optimism was obviously forced. "We still need more of you. Many more. This is a chance of a lifetime, a chance to serve your country, to put to the best possible use all the skills you've learned over the last few weeks. That's right!" Two more men stepped forward. "Don't let your comrades down." He waited.

"Major." The colonel stood beside the commanding officer. "Perhaps they still don't understand. Lads, your country is depending on you. Your comrades in the Niagara area are depending on you. Are you going to let them down? We need sixty more men, now, before time runs out." He faced them, a challenge in every line of his body, apparent even in the darkness. No one moved.

Then, from somewhere in the shadowed ranks, a voice spoke up hesitantly.

"Sir, when we joined the militia we were assured it was for service in our own country only, that we would not have to leave, to go on foreign soil. We will defend our country against invaders, but we will not leave it."

"This is intolerable!" Malachi Jackson was almost dancing with indignation. "Sir, you are a colonel. You can *order* them to go."

"No, Mr. Jackson, I cannot." Lieutenant-Colonel Van Rensselaer was controlling his anger with an effort. "Whoever spoke up is quite right. I cannot order them to go. They are militia, not regulars." He raised his voice. "That is why we are calling for volunteers, sixty more men brave enough to go –"

"Sir, it is not a matter of bravery." A sergeant spoke up. "Let the enemy invade and these men will prove their bravery beyond question. But," he shrugged, "they will not leave their own country."

"I see. Men, is that your final word? You refuse to go?" There was another long moment of silence, broken only by the shuffling of feet and nervous coughs. Then one word was spoken, taken up defiantly by all those who had not moved in answer to the challenge. "YES!"

"I can't believe it!" Malachi's voice shook with frustration. "A glorious opportunity lost because soldiers refuse to fight."

"Believe it, Mr. Jackson." The colonel spoke bitterly. "These men have not suffered from the British blockade as have the Kentuckians, nor suffered savage attacks by Indians egged on by our enemies, as have the people of Indiana or Michigan. They have neither the professionalism of the regular soldier or a hatred of the enemy that outright war demands. They are within their rights. If they refuse to go there is nothing we can do about it. Major Wilson, the project is cancelled."

And he added to no one in particular, "I have never been so humiliated in my life."

* * *

Jared hoped in vain that no one would see the tears in his eyes. His father saw them, and put a reassuring arm around his son's shoulders.

"Don't be disappointed, my boy. Sooner or later these men will come to their senses. There will be many more such opportunities before this war is over."

"Yes, sir." Thank God his father didn't realize that they were tears of relief.

Chapter Seven

Except for one day a week, when they underwent a superficial military training, the war made little difference to the lives of Thomas and James Shaw. The work on the farms in the area continued as before, and the summer passed uneventfully.

Once a week the part-time soldiers of the militia mustered on the square in front of the fort, armed with the Brown Bess musket and fifteen-inch bayonet. They watched in awe as the regulars performed precision drills and executed battlefield manoeuvres and formations, but their training consisted of mastering the musket.

There was more to this, as James found out, than aiming and pulling the trigger. To load, he had to bite off the end of a cartridge and pour a little of the powder into the firing pan, then the remainder down the barrel. This was followed by the ball and wadding, all tamped down with the ramrod. Pulling the trigger activated a flint that ignited the powder. The result was a satisfying flame, smoke and bang that sent the ball out of the muzzle toward the enemy.

All this took time, and even an expert could hope to fire no more than two rounds per minute. James was no expert. Formations were designed so that some men were firing while others were reloading. But for individual 'skirmishes,' which was all the militia was being trained for so far, an attack would probably give the defender time to reload no more than once, then he would have to resort to the bayonet. James and his father desperately hoped that the call to arms would never come.

They were to be disappointed.

First came news of an unexpected victory by General Brock over superior American forces and the capture of far-off Detroit, followed by the encouraging news of a truce. But this was used by both sides to strengthen their forces for the showdown that was coming in the Niagara area. And the battle for control of the St. Lawrence was on.

The summons came in the dark hours of early morning. Thudding hooves on the road and then a sharp rap on the door awakened Thomas.

"Mr. Shaw! You are to muster at the fort immediately. Do you hear?"

"Yes." Thomas bolted upright. "I hear you."

"Right." The sound of hooves diminished rapidly.

Thomas Shaw tried to edge out of bed without waking his wife, but she sat up and passed her hands through thick, tumbled hair.

"I heard, Thomas." She reached out and caught his

hand in a brief clasp, then released it. "Do you think it is an invasion?"

"I expect so." He was pulling on his clothes. "They will want to come now before the fort is complete. I am surprised they have waited so long."

"Then you must hurry." She hesitated. "Must James go?"

"Yes, dear. He must."

She nodded. "I will waken him."

But there was no need. James appeared at their door, his head emerging from his shirt as he pulled it down. "I heard," he said. "I will be in the kitchen."

They gathered there, briefly, in their everyday clothes, for there were still no uniforms available. For a moment Rachel and Thomas clung to each other, then she opened her arms to James. "God go with you, laddie," she whispered. "I will be praying for you."

"I know you will, Mother."

She let them go reluctantly.

They slipped the canoe into the water and paddled swiftly, hugging the shore, peering into the darkness and straining their ears for some indication as to what lay ahead. For some time there was only the rippling and gurgling of the water, disturbed by boat and paddle.

James' mind was in turmoil. So he was going to have to fight! Was he really going to have to try to kill another human being, to fire a musket ball or, worse still, stab with a bayonet? He shuddered at the thought. And Jared – where was he? Was he coming with the invaders? He had said that, as a drummer boy, he would not be expected to fight. But wasn't that how orders were given on the battle-field – by drum beats and rolls? So he would have to be there. Desperately James shut all thoughts of Jared from his mind. He was going to repel an enemy who was threat-ening his home. Nothing more.

At last they saw the winking pinpoint of light which was the enemy's sentry fire on the ramparts across the river. If there was any unusual activity there, it was lost in the darkness.

Surely, thought James, we should be able to see the boats by now, loaded with the invaders. But there was nothing.

Then, as they rounded a wooded point of land, they saw their own fires atop the black bulk of the ramparts. Below them, on the water, they could make out dark shapes, which had to be boats – dozens, maybe hundreds, of boats.

James' first reaction was that they were too late, that the invasion had already taken place. Then he realized his mistake. His father put it into words.

"They're ours!" he said. "*We're* the ones who are going to invade!"

And he was right. He could see now a mass of men drawn up on the square below the fort, the fire winking now and then off fixed bayonets. It was the so-called redcoats, although many of the regiments represented wore blue or, like the Glengarries, green.

They pulled the canoe onto dry ground and paused for a moment. Thomas clasped James' hand.

"Are you afraid, James?"

The boy nodded, tight-lipped.

"So am I. But we're fighting to defend our homes. And your mother and sister. If that means going onto enemy soil to silence their guns, so be it. I know," he added, seeing even in the darkness the haunted look in James' eyes, "it's hard to think of the people of Ogdensburg as 'enemies', but that's what we must do or our hearts won't be in it. Pray God your friend Jared will be safe and leave it in His hands. Come, lad."

"Stand where you are!" A soldier suddenly appeared out of the shadows, challenging them. "Who are you?"

"Militia. Thomas and James Shaw."

"Right. Thomas, report to the armory for your kit. James, you are to come with me. Captain MacKessock wants a word with you."

"With *me*? Why me? You must mean my father." Though why either of them would be singled out was beyond him.

"No. He said, 'James Shaw, the boy' plain enough. Come along."

"Go with him, lad. He may have some special task for you."

James could guess what his father was thinking. He was to be kept out of the fighting because of his age. He hardly knew whether to be relieved or disappointed.

56

"This way."

He followed the soldier into the as yet unfinished blockhouse. Here the quartermaster was handing out muskets, bayonets and cartridge belts under hanging storm lanterns. James was led on to an inner door. His guide rapped on it.

"James Shaw is here, sir."

"Show him in."

Captain MacKessock was there, and James recognized, with a shock, the other man who was with him. Colonel 'Red George' Macdonell of the Glengarries.

"You...you wanted to see me, sir?"

"Yes, James, I do." He turned to the colonel. "This is the boy I was speaking of."

"All right, Archie. It's your show. Go ahead." He turned to James, looking him quickly up and down. "Good luck, my boy."

James managed a faint, "Thank you, sir," before the colonel nodded to the captain and went out.

"Now, James," said Captain MacKessock, "you told me, when we first met, that you are a friend of Malachi Jackson and his family. Is that not right?"

"Yes, sir." James was thoroughly mystified.

"And you know where he lives – where his house is located? Good. As you must have guessed by now, we are going over the river to silence their guns. It's something that must be done. But we have no quarrel with the good people of Ogdensburg and wish to cause as little harm to and bad feelings with the townsfolk as possible. Malachi

Jackson has a lot of influence over the people of the town. I have here," he patted a pouch on his belt,"a message for Mr. Jackson that I want you to deliver once we have achieved our objective. Understand? When we reach the far shore, I want you to stay with your boat, no matter what happens, until I send for you. That way I'll know where to find you when the time comes." He looked questioningly at James. "Do I make myself clear?"

"Yes, sir."

"Good. Since you're going to be my envoy, you will need some identification other than what you're wearing. This should fit reasonably well."

He turned and took a military jacket from a peg. It was green, with black collar and cuffs, and three rows of white buttons down the front of the breast.

"I haven't any uniform trousers but your own will do fine. Now this." And he took from another peg a high shako of black felt with the crest of the Glengarries on the crown. "Try it on."

James put the items of clothing on, his mind numb at this unexpected turn of events. They fit reasonably well. Captain MacKessock, himself in scarlet, a true redcoat, nodded in satisfaction.

"Good. Now I must go and have a word with the militia. They and your father will be in the rear and may not have to leave their boats if the regulars do the job. But they will be there if needed. I may be a while. Have a seat and wait here till I return."

James waited for what seemed like hours, listening to the sounds from outside of orders given in hushed tones, of men moving about, of feet tramping in unison. He wondered how hundreds of men could embark in darkness without total confusion. But that wasn't his problem. And he thought of the role he was to play – to wait safely in the boat until word came, then go openly to the Jackson's home as an envoy with a message. He hated the thought of facing Malachi Jackson in the role of victor. The man would be resentful, to say the least. But that couldn't be helped. The important thing was that he might catch at least a glimpse of Leah, that he might even have a chance to speak to her. James smiled. And she'd see him in his odd half-uniform.

With the guns at Ogdensburg silenced, was it possible that the old peaceful relations between the two towns could be restored? Was that what the message for Malachi was about? If so, Mr. Jackson would never go for it. But it was worth a try.

"Right, James. Come with me. It will soon be dawn. If the enemy doesn't know by now what we're planning, he soon will. We can expect a warm reception."

Of course. Those guns could do a lot of damage, a lot of killing, before they were captured. At any moment now they could be expected to open fire. And how could the enemy miss that mass of boats soon to be underway? James was aware of sweat running down his arm, and it wasn't because of the warmth of his jacket.

He followed the captain and was surprised to see how order had come out of confusion. The regulars were already afloat, and the last of the militia were filing into the big batteau, each with a musket and cartridge belt, and a bayonet on the hip. And he realized that he could see what was going on much clearer than he could when he and his father arrived at Prescott. Pale light was reaching into the sky.

Captain MacKessock led the way to where a naval cutter was tied up to the jetty. Eight sailors sat rigidly, their oars held vertically as if they were presenting arms.

"James, take your place in the stern. And remember, stay there until I summon you."

"Yes, sir."

The captain took his place in the bow. Someone on the shore released the lines. A petty officer pushed the cutter clear with a boat hook. "Ready, sir?"

"Yes. Let's go."

The oars came down in unison, dipped into the water and sent the cutter swiftly down an avenue between the heavily laden boats. The open water lay ahead.

The captain, in the bow, looked back with satisfaction as the armada began to move. There were a few minor collisions, a few muffled curses in the darkness. Then the flotilla was under way, a huge black mass moving out onto the river.

James wasn't looking back. He looked first to the east, where the sky was growing steadily lighter and then ahead where dark shapes were becoming distinguishable …the ramparts, the guns…

Any minute now those guns would open fire. The enemy must have known for some time what was coming. What were they waiting for? The gunners must be standing to their weapons, just waiting for the order to fire.

There had been a gunboat at Prescott some weeks earlier, James remembered, but it had been called away. We need it now, he thought, to draw the enemy's fire, to challenge their guns. As it was, the men in the boats could do nothing to protect themselves until they were within musket range. If they got that far.

He could only wait, sitting there in the stern with sweaty palms and a cold feeling in his gut as the sailors, in perfect unison, sent the cutter into the lead. With their backs to the bow they couldn't see what lay ahead – breastworks taking shape out of the fading darkness, topped by the menacing, unmistakable shapes of heavy cannon.

What was it like for the men behind those guns, watching a vast invading force emerging from the darkness, waiting with forced patience for the order to fire?

James glanced back. The cutter seemed to be moving too fast, leaving an open swath between it and the cumbersome, heavily laden boats. What was the captain planning? A mad, solo dash for victory or a hero's death?

The captain saw the danger too. At a low command the sailors ceased their rowing, oars horizontal, dripping water, while the gap closed. Then they carried on a slower pace. Still the guns were silent.

They're asleep, thought James. They haven't even seen us. We're going to capture the guns without a shot being fired.

And then his dream was shattered. First, a drum beat was carried distinctly across the water. Jared! thought James. Jared's awake at least. But there was no more time to think of Jared.

Then a sheet of flames came from the ramparts, followed by a cloud of rolling smoke, and the deafening crash of twenty-four pounders thundering out their challenge.

Petrified, James could only watch in fascination for the cannon balls, and he saw them coming, passing overhead like a rushing wind, to fall somewhere behind. Overshot. Then the guns at Fort Wellington replied with a raging thunder that assaulted the ears and numbed the brain.

And then a different sound, and he knew that their mortars had opened up. He saw the shot climb high, iron balls falling, growing and blossoming, and canisters bursting, raining death on the boats below. Columns of water were flung up to hang on the air. But not all fell in the water. Boats were shattered, oars smashed, bodies dismembered, blood ran and men died.

Still the boats came on, those unharmed pushing past their unlucky comrades, leaving them for the trailing doctor's boat to care for.

His father! Where was he? He must still be safe. The militia's boats in the rear would have escaped the bombardment. So far. But they were coming on, right into the path of destruction. Unless the gunners altered their range the next salvo would hit them. But then the lead boats would be in the clear. The enemy wouldn't want that to happen. At least there would be a lull while they reloaded.

But he was wrong. Apparently not all the guns had opened fire at once. Now, while they were reloading, others belched out their load of death. More balls and canisters were coming. James saw them.

But he didn't see the one that hit the cutter. He was only aware of shattered wood, a suddenly headless body, screams of pain and spurting blood. Something smashed into him, knocking the breath out of him. Something else slashed him across the head. Then nothing.

Chapter Eight

J ames' head seemed to be floating independently of his body – the wierdest sensation – and his eyelids were heavy, too heavy to move. He lay still, waiting for his head to behave, then he gradually became aware that something strange was going on.

This was not his bed. This one was wide and deep and very comfortable, not like his own narrow cot and lumpy mattress. There was the faintest hint of lilacs in the air, and that was ridiculous. The lilac season was long past

He listened. Birds were singing and there were chickens somewhere nearby outside. That was normal. But then a clock struck – a deep, booming chime tolling out the hours. He had never heard one like that before. He tried to count the strokes, but lost count. It was at least ten o'clock, maybe eleven, or even twelve. And in the morning too. Even with his eyes closed he was well aware that it was broad daylight. He should have been up and at work hours ago.

He forced his eyes open. Sun was streaming through a window with lace curtains. His own curtains were strips

of flour sacking, bleached and scrubbed to a shiny whiteness, but still flour sacking. And there was wallpaper here,
not the bare logs he was used to. It was a pale yellow with
tiny red roses all over it, and there was a picture hanging
there, of a basket of flowers.

He moved his head carefully. He saw a piece of furniture, richly stained, with curving legs and a tall mirror –
nothing like the rough but serviceable chest of drawers
his father had made for him. And what on earth was that
up there, in front of the mirror? A doll! Of all things, a doll,
with tight blond curls and a white satin dress.

It had to be a dream, but not like anything he had ever
dreamed before. And there was still that faint hint of
lilac. Could you *dream* a perfume like that? He moved
his head a little more, and then he knew for sure it was a
dream.

Leah Jackson was there, sitting in a chair, very still, the
only movement the gentle rise and fall of her breast as she
slept. There was a red rose in her black hair that fell in
rich waves to her shoulders, pushed back behind her
small ears, and her long lashes lay against her cheeks.
There was color in her cheeks and in her slightly parted
lips…. Oh yes, he had dreamed like this before.

She opened her eyes. She was looking at him, momentarily confused. Then her face lit up in glad surprise.

"Jamie!" She was out of her chair and coming toward
him and the hint of lilacs came with her. He remembered
another occasion when he had been an awkward guest at

a party in the Jackson's home. She had been there, breath-takingly beautiful with a suggestion of lilacs about her.

She leaned over him, wonderfully close, adjusting a cover, and he knew in awed wonder that it was no dream.

"Jamie," she said again. "Thank God you're better."

Better? Had he been ill?

"Leah," he said, but the name stuck in his throat. "Leah," he tried again, "Where am I?"

"You're in my bed," she said softly. "You have been for nearly a month."

In *her* bed! In the Jackson's beautiful home! Desperately he tried to make sense out of it. Something was coming back – memories of an armada of bateaus and hundreds of soldiers, of cannon balls and screams and a river of blood. And his mission – to take a message to the Jackson's home. Was that why he was here? Had the Glengarries captured the guns? Had he carried out his mission, and somehow it had all been blotted from his memory? That would explain his presence here...except, why in bed? And she had said, almost a month!

"Leah," he said, "I don't understand. Why am I here? What happened?"

"We found you," she explained. "Washed up on the riverbank after your boats were driven back. You had a concussion and a fever." Her hand was on his forehead, wonderfully gentle and cool. "We didn't think you would live." There were tears in her dark eyes. She blinked them away. "That was nearly four weeks ago."

"Four weeks!" He tried to make sense of it, then a sudden thought jolted him. "My parents!"

"Don't fret," she said quickly. "They know. We sent word to them. Father made sure of that. I think," she said, with a little smile, "he was proud to have a prisoner. And now we can let them know that you're out of danger. And you don't have to worry about your father either. His boat wasn't hit."

"His boat! Oh yes...what happened? We failed? We never captured the guns?"

"No. Your army never reached land. Father or Jared can tell you all about it. They were there. Mother and I just heard the guns. And oh, Jamie, maybe I shouldn't be, but I'm glad it worked out the way it did. Because now you won't have to fight anymore and I won't have to worry about you."

"You would worry? About me?" Leah, beautiful Leah, daughter of a well-to-do lawyer, worrying about him, James Shaw! It was incredible.

"Of course," she said, simply. "Now I'm going to call the doctor. I think he's still in the house. He was about to have a cup of tea when I fell asleep." She gently but firmly pushed him back when he tried to rise. "Lie still. I won't be a minute."

He watched her go, wonderment in his heart. Strange how things had worked out. He had looked forward to a quick visit to this house, delivering a message to Mr. Jackson, hoping for at best a glimpse, a brief word with

Leah. And now here he was in her room, and she cared about him and was glad that he wouldn't fight anymore.

Wouldn't he? What was his position, anyway? He had washed up on enemy territory, and that would make him a prisoner of war. So he should be in a prison camp hospital instead of here in the lap of luxury. Mr. Jackson must have used his influence. Mr. Jackson, who had forbidden his children to associate with the 'enemy?' But things were different now. James was the defeated enemy – a prisoner – and Mr. Jackson could afford to be magnanimous. James was now the symbol of an American victory.

The doctor came in, followed by Leah and Mrs. Jackson. While they stood aside he felt James' head, took his temperature, listened to his heart and beamed with satisfaction.

"We've won," he said, turning to the ladies. "We've licked the fever, his head is mended and he's well on his way to recovery." He turned to James. "You're a lucky young man. These two ladies have nursed you and cooled your fever and prayed over you and saved your life. In a few days you will be as good as new."

"Thank... thank you." He tried to find words to express his gratitude but none came. "Why have you been so good to me? I should be just a prisoner of war."

Mrs. Jackson smiled. "You *are* a prisoner, James, as Malachi reminds us, but you're a special friend of Jared and Leah, and we wouldn't dream of leaving you to the mercies of an army doctor and a prison camp."

"But why here? Why in Leah's room? I shouldn't have put her out."

"You didn't have any say in the matter, did you? Leah has spent the most time with you, changing the dressing, keeping you cooled down when the fever raged. She wanted you to be in here. She has a comfortable chair to sleep in, and when it's my turn, she sleeps in the spare room. You were no bother, James."

No bother! He had to laugh at that. "I *was* a bother. A big nuisance. And I'm so grateful. What…what happens now? What happens when I'm well again?"

"I don't know," admitted Mrs. Jackson. "That's up to Malachi. He had permission to keep you here until you recovered, but after that, I don't know. He will come in to see you when he returns tomorrow. He will be pleased to see you are well again."

"Right," said the doctor, replacing his instruments in his bag. "I think what the boy needs now is a good meal – he's as thin as a rake – and then some sleep. And maybe tomorrow we'll have him on his feet for a few minutes at least."

"Of course," said Mrs. Jackson. "It will take only a few minutes to prepare some chicken broth. Come, Leah."

"Yes, Mother." And then, in front of her mother and the doctor, she leaned over and kissed James, quickly, on his brow. And then was gone.

* * *

"Well, my boy, I'm pleased to see you have recovered."
Malachi Jackson towered over James at the bedside, his
hands clasped behind his back. "This is very satisfactory.
Jared and Leah have been great friends of yours and it has
been difficult for them to think of you as the enemy."

"Thank you, sir. And thanks for arranging for me to stay
here. Can you tell me what happened when we…when
your guns fired on our boats? I was in a cutter that was hit
early and I don't know what happened after that."

"Oh yes." Mr. Jackson recalled the action with satisfaction. "Our gunners held their fire until you were well
within range of our mortars and then blasted your boats
out of the water. You never got more than half way. We
did so much damage, you had to give up and turn back.
Our militia proved themselves that day, my boy. It was
their first action, and they came through."

"Were there any other prisoners taken besides me?"

"No. We didn't follow up by going after you, although
we could have." He evidently thought that was a mistake.
"We don't know what happened to you. Your men must
have pulled the rest of your dead and wounded from the
water, but somehow they missed you. And that afternoon
Leah found you on the riverbank."

"*Leah* did?"

"Yes. She was out walking and she literally stumbled
over you. You are a prisoner, of course, but I was able to
persuade the authorities to let you recover here, for Leah
and Jared's sake.

Now you are very fortunate. For you, of course, the war is over."

"Yes, I guess it is." He *was* lucky, he reflected. He had never wanted to fight. Now he wouldn't have to. His conscience would be clear. You can't fight behind bars – for he couldn't expect to be kept here much longer. And there would be no more worries about meeting Jared in combat.

"What happens now?" he ventured. "Will I go to a prison camp?"

"Well, that's up to you." Mr. Jackson was looking at him keenly.

"What do you mean, sir?"

"You have two choices. You can go to prison camp and remain there for the duration. That's one option. Or you can stay right here."

"Here!" He stared at Mr. Jackson. "Here? In your home? With…" he was going to say with Leah, but thought better of it. "…with your family? How could that be? I'm still the enemy. I don't understand."

"It can happen. All you have to do is promise never to take up arms against the United States of America again. That's it. Your father is a man of honor and I have no doubt you are too. I will take your word on it. Promise that, and you can stay here. And when the opportunity arises and you are fully recovered, we will see that you get home. But of course you must remember your word will be as binding there as it is here. That is your choice. Your promise never to fight us again, and stay here, or go to prison."

Choice? Was there really a choice? This place of comfort, and friends, and good food, against life in a prison camp.

"I'm going to leave you now to think it over," said Malachi. "I will be back in two hours for your decision."

What was there to think over? He would be a fool to give this up. He could stay here until he was completely recovered, and then go home where his parents must be waiting anxiously for him. Yes, he wanted to go back, back to his father and mother and little sister, to their love and their handmade home, to the toil out in the open air, with the animals and the birds, the hard won harvests and the river rolling past their clearing....

And all he had to do was promise not to fight again. What could be easier? He didn't want to fight anyway. What fighting was there likely to be in the future for the militia? One attempt to silence the American guns had failed. If there was another one, he wouldn't have to go. His father would though. James would have to stay at home. And hope. And pray....

Or perhaps it would be the Americans' turn next to invade, and his home would be in danger, his family in peril. War turned some ordinary people into little more than demons – he knew that. He could see them, enemy troops, ravaging his home, brutalizing his mother and sister while he stood by, helpless, bound by an oath not to fight....

Perhaps there *was* something to think over.

* * *

Malachi Jackson came back into the room. Leah was with him. Her eyes met James' and there was pleading there. She wants me to stay, he thought in wonder. How can I refuse?

"Well, boy, have you decided?"

"Yes, I have. Mr. Jackson, suppose it was the other way around. If it was Jared in my position...if he had to choose between being a prisoner or living in luxury simply by refusing to fight for his country. How would you expect him to choose?"

"I would expect him," said Mr. Jackson, "to choose prison. I would be ashamed of him otherwise."

James nodded. He didn't look at Leah. "Then you have my answer, sir. I cannot promise not to fight for my country anymore."

"As you wish." There was respect in Malachi's voice, but there was also cold decision. "You will go to the army doctor tomorrow, and he will decide when you can be moved to a prison camp. Come, Leah."

"Leah!" There was pleading in *his* gaze now. He reached out a hand to her.

She looked at him, ignoring his hand, stony-faced.

"Please," he whispered. "Try to understand."

She shook her head. "I don't understand any of this," she said bleakly. She turned and went out after her father.

Chapter Nine

"You know you are a fool, James." Jared was speaking to him through the bars of the cell in which James was held awaiting passage to a prisoner-of-war camp.

James looked up at his friend from the cot which was the only furniture provided.

"Why do you say that, Jared?"

"It's obvious. You're here," he indicated the bare cell, "and in a day or two you'll be taken under guard to a prison camp, and you won't be any better off there than you are here. Worse, in fact. Here you've got friends who can come to visit you, but I hear they're taking you all the way to Plattsburg. And instead of that, you could be in our house in comfort."

"I suppose you would have chosen differently," said James dryly.

"Oh no. I'm a fool too. I admit that." Jared grinned. "I would have done the same thing. We're both fools, so I understand why you did what you did."

"I don't think Leah understands," said James gloomily.

"No, she doesn't, even though she's in love with you. Or maybe that's why."

James wasn't listening. In love with him! The dream, the hope suddenly put into stark words, took his breath away. Yes, back there in her room he had dared to hope that she was in love with him. But not now.

"If only she would let me explain. But she wouldn't even see me again."

"No, she's crying her eyes out. And you can hardly blame her. She saved your life and you left her for this!"

"But I'm sure she would understand if she would only give me a chance."

"Not her," said Jared airily. "Women don't understand war."

"Maybe they *do* understand war, better than we do. They understand it means killing and maiming instead of talking and bargaining."

"Now you're talking like a woman. That's what comes of being in love."

"Who said *I'm* in love?"

"Your face says so. You know you might as well have made that promise. As a prisoner, you'll not have a chance to fight again anyway."

"Oh, you never know. There's such a thing as prisoner exchange."

"Oh yes, I've heard of that. But that's reserved for officers or disabled men who'll never fight again anyway.

Why would anyone trade for you? You're the only prisoner *we've* got, and, as far as I know, your side hasn't any… not over there in Prescott anyway. No one we're likely to want in exchange for you."

"Thanks a lot," said James dryly. "You sure know how to cheer a fellow up."

"Sorry, James," said Jared contritely. "But that's the way it is. At least as a prisoner you'll be fed…not like you would in our home, but you'll get *something*. And you won't have to fight again. Know something, James? I was afraid you and I might meet in battle and we would have to try to kill each other…and I don't think I could do that."

"*You* were afraid of that? So was I. I still am. Because it could happen yet."

"How? You're going to a prison in Plattsburg, James. You're out of it for good."

"Unless," said James slowly, "unless I escape."

"Escape!" Jared stared, then grinned. "By George, you're just the chap to do it. Too bad I can't help you. But I wouldn't be surprised, James, if you pull it off. Maybe you *will* fight again. Forgive me, but I hope you fail. I'd much rather know you're a prisoner. And so would Leah."

Chapter Ten

It was cold in the cell. Heat from the iron stove in the guard's outer room barely reached in through the iron bars. His Glengarry jacket had been taken away to hang as a souvenir in the guard room, but they brought him a great coat, patched and frayed, though thick and warm. His was a face familiar to many of the town's people, for they had seen him often enough with the Jackson children. They visited him, bringing him little extras while bemoaning the war. Best of all they brought some candles whose meagre flames helped to warm his hands.

He learned, in a roundabout way, that an American force had suffered a setback – not a defeat, he was assured, but admittedly a setback – when their invasion of Canada had been repulsed at a place called Queenston in the Niagara area. But General Brock, believed to be the only competent general on the Canadian side, had been killed, so American victory was just a question of time. Then James would be free again. Meantime, for him the war was over.

Mr. Jackson came to see him to make sure he was being treated according to army regulations. He was the one who made sure the coat was provided, for winter was fast approaching and the cell was cold. If civilians wanted to add a few luxuries to make James' conditions a little more endurable, that was their concern and fine with him. Soon James would be taken away to a proper war prison, and then he would be beyond the help of his friends.

Mrs. Jackson came to see him, with some freshly baked bread, and wished the war would end.

Jared came to see him – to see, he said, if James had managed to escape yet. Escape from the fort, he said confidently, was impossible. James would have to wait until he was transferred to a prison camp. There at least he would be in the company of others like him, some of whom would likely have similar ideas. But Jared doubted if James or anyone else would succeed. James had his own thoughts about that.

Leah didn't come to see him. And, for some reason, James didn't ask about her.

* * *

The transfer came as the month of November reached its median, with slate gray skies and cold, snow-bearing winds. They took him out, hands bound, escorted by four soldiers and a sergeant who marched him to the water-front where a large whaler-type rowboat awaited them.

"We're taking you to Plattsburg," he was informed.

"About forty miles or so by river, then across country. You will take your turn rowing, when your hands will be free but your feet bound. For the first watch, take your place in the bow."

So he sat with both hands and feet bound while the whaler pushed off from the wharf with the four soldiers pulling on the oars, their backs to him. The sergeant sat at the tiller, facing him, watching him.

But James was paying no attention to his guard. He was looking across the gray, wind-ruffled water to Prescott, to the imposing structure of the fort, to the guns on the battlements. Perhaps this was the day the militia would be training there. Was his father there? Was he the only one giving a thought to the sole prisoner taken on that aborted attempt to silence the American guns? Was there someone watching the departure of this whaler through a telescope, perhaps mildly interested, not particularly worried about six men in a boat?

James was concerned. If he was to escape it would have to be soon. The very words 'prison camp' seemed to him to spell the end of hope.

But right now the river was cold. He wasn't a good swimmer anyway, even with free hands and feet, and the sergeant was facing him with a pistol in his belt. James would have to bide his time.

Aided by the current, the whaler soon left Ogdensburg and Prescott behind. There was no one to observe them, so they kept to the middle of the river to take advantage of the current. James took turns rowing with the four privates, amused by their complaints that they had joined the army, not the navy. But James found himself disheartened. He was always bound either hand or foot or both, and by the sergeant's watchful eyes.

Once they rested on their oars to pass around the water bottle and eat some hard biscuits. James was given a full share but it wasn't much. It wasn't until the afternoon was waning, and some thought must soon be given to their plans for the night, that there was any hint of a break in their routine.

Sergeant Hare had been studying the Canadian shore for some time.

"There, lads," he said at last, pointing. "There's a tidy little house and a prosperous-looking homestead. What do you bet he's one of them traitor Tories who refused to fight for a free country against the Britishers? I reckon he owes us a little something. What do you say to a good fat Canadian chicken for our pot?"

"What do you mean, sarge?"

"What I say. We're going to ask him politely to give us one of his chickens for our ease and comfort. Perhaps one would not do. Two, then. And some fresh milk, of course."

"What if he refuses?"

"Ha!" grinned the sergeant. Apparently he hoped the farmer would object. "Then we will have to teach him and his family, supposing he has one, some manners, won't we?"

"How will we do that?" The speaker sounded uneasy.

"Oh, we'll think of something, don't you worry. Keep rowing, my lads." The sergeant moved the tiller so that they were heading for shore.

James, who was one of the rowers, turned his head in an effort to see what had attracted the sergeant's attention.

"You! Prisoner! Eyes front! Pick up the pace, lads. It looks like a sloping shore. We'll run the boat up the bank. One! Two! That's it."

The whaler surged ahead as they picked up the tempo. James could only guess what lay ahead. Probably a farm much like the Shaws', with chickens, a cow or two, pigs perhaps, just beginning to show the results of hard work and sacrifice.

"We're just about there. Brace yourselves. Brooke," he said to the man in the bow, "jump ashore with the painter as soon as we hit."

The keel hit bottom, and the whaler ran up the bank and ground to a halt, half out of the water.

"Good," approved the sergeant. "Right, lads, down oars. My friend here," he tapped the butt of a pistol in his belt, "will be all the persuasion we need."

"What about the prisoner?" asked the soldier who shared a thwart with James. "His feet are tied."

"Lash his hands as well. That will immobilize him. Stay with him for a minute, Brooke, while I survey the situation. Then we'll see what we can liberate from these Tories."

James obediently held his hands and wrists close together in front of him. The man Brooke lashed his wrists with a rope, rather apologetically, though he said nothing. *In front of him*! James watched the sergeant, breath suspended. The NCO was paying no attention...

As James had guessed, this was a farm much like the Shaws', with sturdy log buildings. Chickens strutted and pecked but there was no sign of human life.

Sergeant Hare studied the situation for a moment. The house was set back among some trees. He turned.

"Brooke! Leave the prisoner. He's not going anywhere. Bring two muskets. You and Archer go around..." he waved his arm in a circular motion..."to the front of the house. Or is it the back? Who cares? There'll be a door there anyway. If and when I give a double whistle, it will be because I'm being threatened. You go in through the house and take them from the rear."

"Right, sarge."

And James was left alone. It was awkward, but the rope binding his feet was low enough on his ankles that he was able to part his knees wide enough to let his bound wrists through between them, so his fingers could reach the rope and work at the knot. If he could free his feet, he could at least run. His hands? He would have to worry about that later.

The sergeant and two men walked openly toward the house, while Brooke and Archer circled into the trees. They had gone only a few steps when Sergeant Hare held up his hand to stop them. "Hear that? There's pigs here too. Pork for the taking for the rest of our journey. The sound's coming from that barn..." He stopped. There came a sudden angry barking from inside the house. The door opened. A man stood there, a gun under his arm, a snarling dog straining on a leash.

"What do you want?" The man watched them suspiciously, holding the dog back.

"Food," said the sergeant easily. His hand hovered over the butt of his pistol. "I believe we'll take a hen or two, and if you have a small suckling pig –"

"No!" The man stepped forward, threateningly. The dog growled low in his throat and bared his teeth. "We don't do business with Yankee soldiers."

"Who said anything about doing business? This is strictly give and take. You give, we take. We'll just take what we need and thank you very much."

"Oh, no you won't." Things happened very quickly then. The dog yanked its leash free of the man's grasp and hurtled across the intervening space, fangs bared. The sergeant waited calmly, then at the last moment, when he couldn't miss, he pulled the trigger. The dog seemed to hang in mid air, writhing and twisting, then fell dead at their feet.

With an oath the man raised his gun. The sergeant whistled sharply, an odd, double whistle. There was the sound of hurried movement in the house, of furniture being overturned, of a woman's scream. The man swung round. Before he knew what was happening, a woman was pushed through the door, falling against him, knocking his gun aside, stumbling, falling at his feet. Two men were grabbing him, overpowering him, taking his gun, throwing him to the ground beside the woman. From inside came the high-pitched cry of a little child.

Sergeant Hare and his men encircled the fallen couple.

"Stay there," he growled. "Don't move and no harm will come to you. Men, round up a couple of hens and a pig."

"My baby!" The woman was looking up at him, her face pale, her eyes snapping. "I must go to my baby."

"Ten minutes. That's all we'll take. Your brat will be all right for ten minutes. Just you stay quiet if you don't want it harmed."

"You beast!"

But the sergeant just laughed. He turned to his men. "Come on. It shouldn't take long. Where's Brooke? Keep an eye on these two. Archer, come with me. We'll see what's in the pig pen. You others pick out a couple of fat hens."

James was paying no attention to what was going on. His fingers worked awkwardly, fumbling at the knotted rope around his ankles. At last it gave. His feet were free! His first impulse was to run, anywhere, away from his captors. But on second thought he knew that would be a mistake. He could hardly hope to outrun the soldiers even if they didn't bring him down with their muskets. There had to be a better way. He looked around desperately. There must be something...there! The oar lock. The metal plate that held it in position was bent up. And it was sharp. He crouched, his body hiding his actions from those on shore. He didn't dare look back to see if he had been seen. Holding his breath, he worked the rope back and forth across the metal. It was very small. There wasn't much room to work. But it was his only hope. Back and forth, barking his knuckles on the gunwale. Back and forth. It frayed. One strand broke, but there were more. It seemed to be taking forever. Again and again. Another strand gone. He was sweating in spite of the cold.

He heard a shot behind him. He froze. Had he been caught out? Were they shooting at him? He crouched, expecting a musket ball to slam into his body. But no, that wasn't a musket. It was a pistol. What were they shooting at? He dare not look. One more time. The rope parted. His hands were free!

He turned then. There was a man and woman lying on the ground, covered by Brooke with his musket, and a dead dog lay nearby. That must account for the single shot he had heard. Two of the privates were chasing some squawking hens, and he had a glimpse of the sergeant at the door of one of the out-buildings. They had forgotten him. For the moment.

He sprang ashore. With all his might, he lifted and strained and pushed the heavy whaler until it was afloat. Then he was on board, standing, poling the boat farther out until he was into deep water. Then he sat and caught up two oars and began to row. In a few minutes he would feel the strength of the current coming to his aid. If he was given a few minutes…

Then he was seen. He heard their shouts, saw the two men who were armed run to the shore and take aim. There was nothing he could do except hope and pray they would miss.

Two puffs of smoke. A musket ball sent splinters flying from the gunwale beside him. He heard the other pass his head. But neither hit him. And now they would have to reload. He had made it.

But now what?

He was going downriver. He had no choice. He would never battle the heavy whaler against the current all by himself. And what would his cheated captors do? He saw them, running along the riverbank, keeping him in sight. They would either be there on the bank awaiting him when he eventually landed, or they would find a boat and come after him – and that was only a question of time; everyone who lived by the river had a boat.

No, there was only one thing to do – to at least give them a run for their money before he was recaptured. He would land on the American shore. What he would do then, he could worry about later. His first task must be to put as much distance between him and the American soldiers as possible. He redoubled his efforts on the oars, heading the boat away from his shouting, gesturing guards….

He reached the shore as dusk was settling around him. There was no shelving beach here but an overhanging bank. He stood up, reaching for undergrowth, pulling himself up, kicking free from the boat. It nudged the bank and drifted sideways. He no longer cared. He was on dry land and he was free.

But he was on the wrong side of the river, in enemy territory and a long way from home. And night was falling fast.

Chapter Eleven

I t was cold and yet James was sweating. He wanted to take off his coat and lie down and go to sleep. But he daren't do that. He had to keep moving until he could find some sort of shelter. Was his fever returning? That was what he feared. His coat wouldn't account for this suffocating heat, or the lightness in his head. He must find some place out of reach of the biting wind. But this was enemy territory. He might be accepted if he knocked on a door now, but it was only a question of time, a few hours at the most, before everyone would be on the lookout for an escaped prisoner. A barn, warmed by the body heat of animals, perhaps with a hay mow? That would suffice, though it wouldn't ease the pangs of hunger that were gnawing at his stomach.

He thought longingly of the Jacksons' warm home, of the smell of freshly baked bread, and Leah's cool touch on his hot forehead. And he could be there now, instead of this…but then he remembered a dead dog, and a woman and man lying on the ground under the threatening muzzles of muskets, and he thought, what if that was my parents, and me standing by helpless? And he knew he had done the right thing. But that didn't help his present predicament.

He was walking – stumbling rather – in a westerly direction. He knew he was going the right way because he was keeping the pale sheen of the river on his right, and that was where, eventually, he would find a boat that would take him back across the river. But that would have to wait. He daren't go back on the river now even if he did find a boat. First he had to find some shelter, some place to rest and sleep. There were farms along here, he was pretty sure, and villages. If he could keep going a little longer, one step at a time, and keep praying as he had been taught, something would turn up.

He saw a light. It was a lantern...moving, casting weird, elongated shadows.

He stopped, clinging to a tree for support, and watched the light. It was being carried by a man. He saw now that the man was moving from one dark, shadowed bulk to another similar but larger one. Then another light appeared – a soft, friendly glow in a window. The moving light approached it. A door opened, splashing more light onto the ground. The man went inside. The door closed.

So, thought James hazily, the smaller building must be a barn. If I can reach that....

Moving with great care, setting one foot carefully in front of the other, trying to ignore the dizziness that threatened him, he approached the barn. He saw, with relief, that it was high enough to include a hay mow on the top floor, above the byre. He groped along the wall until he found the door, a heavy latch holding it shut. It seemed like a ton weight, but he managed to lift it, and pull. The hinges groaned. He held his breath, listening. Nothing. He stepped inside. It was pitch black in there, but he heard heavy feet moving on a plank floor, and the snuffling of an animal disturbed in its sleep. Cows, he guessed, gratefully. And maybe pigs. Their body heat was welcome. He moved carefully, feeling his way along a wall, close behind the cows. A switching tail brushed him. He spoke some soft, soothing words. There must be a ladder, he thought. He found it, standing against the wall. He began to climb, one rung at a time, pausing at each one to clear his head, until he reached the top floor. There was hay here, lots of it. He could smell it. He pulled himself away from the gap at the head of the ladder. He was no longer hot. He was shivering. He collapsed in the hay, pulling at it to cover him, passing into nothing.

Something moved across his face. He brushed it away. Something heavy was on his chest. He tried to brush that away too but it wouldn't move. It was thin, hard, and pointed. He opened his eyes. There was a pitch fork held against his chest. There was a man holding it there, towering above him.

For a moment he could only stare stupidly. Then he became aware of the hay all around him, of sunlight finding its way between barn boards and through knot holes, of a million motes of dust dancing in its beams. And he remembered. He looked up at the bearded face staring down at him. Not hostile. James felt a twinge of hope. Not hostile, just wary and curious. But the sharp tines of the fork were still there against his chest.

"Who are you?" The voice was calm but cautious.

"James Shaw." He spoke without thinking. He should have invented another name, but it was too late now.

"And what are you doing, James Shaw, in my hay?"

James took a deep breath. Things were beginning to make sense. He realized with relief that the threatened fever had left him. And the man's attitude suggested that he had not as yet heard of an escaped prisoner.

"Resting," he said. "I got very tired and the hay was inviting. Thank you very much."

"We have beds more comfortable than this hay." The fork hadn't moved. "Why did you not knock on our door?"

"I didn't know I would be welcomed. I didn't want to disturb anyone."

"You're not from these parts or you would know a stranger is never turned away." The grip on the fork relaxed a little, but it was still there. "Where are you from and where are you going?"

"I'm from Plattsburg and I'm going to Ogdensburg to visit friends there."

"Who might these friends be?"

James was glad he was asked about Ogdensburg. He

knew nothing about Plattsburg. "The Jacksons. Malachi Jackson. We're cousins."

"So you're related to Malachi Jackson? Everyone knows him." The man hesitated, then pulled the fork back, plunged it into the hay and left it standing there. He reached out a big, calloused hand.

"I am Hugh MacKinnon. We never turn away strangers in need. I have already asked more questions than is seemly." He caught James' hand and pulled him up. "But in these strange, troubled times it is as well to be careful. I don't know why you are so far off the road to Ogdensburg. You can explain that, if you like, after breakfast. But first, come with me."

Breakfast! James was acutely aware of two things – of a gnawing emptiness in his belly, and a need to get going before Sergeant Hare and his men appeared. Why had they not done so already? Surely they had secured another boat and come after him long before this. His luck could not hold out much longer.

But he must eat no matter what. If he could eat something fast, he might still get away before the soldiers appeared.

But Hugh MacKinnon was in no hurry. "Go you to the kitchen," he said, "and introduce yourself to Lucy – that's my wife. She will set a place for you and I will join you in a few minutes."

The thought persisted that he should just go while the going was good, but his stomach rebelled against that. So he found himself in a low-ceilinged kitchen where a woman, tall and black-haired with cheeks red from the heat of the stove, welcomed him as if his presence was the most natural thing in the world.

"You have slept in our barn," she guessed, noting the wisps of hay still clinging to his clothes. "That is too bad. We have a good spare bed since our boy left. But of course you wouldn't know that. I am Lucy. Hugh told you to come in for breakfast. Is that right?"

"Yes. I'm James Shaw. And I want to thank you…"

"No need. We're pleased to share the goodness God has blessed us with. Would you like to wash? You will find soap and a towel in there, and I will put more eggs in the pan."

So in a few minutes James was sitting down to a plate of eggs and bacon and potatoes, with milk fresh from the cows. He wanted to dig right in but Hugh MacKinnon held up a hand.

"First we must give thanks," he said, and he opened a big Bible at the Twenty-third Psalm. James listened impatiently to the familiar words until one sentence seemed to spring out at him from utter silence.

Thou preparest a table before me in the presence of mine enemies.

James looked sharply at his host. If only he knew how appropriate those words were! But Mr. MacKinnon apparently noticed no special significance. He continued to read but James didn't hear any more of it. He was thinking, perhaps it wasn't just luck that had brought him here.

The food was delicious. James had to force himself to eat slowly, keeping pace with his host and hostess. Hugh was in no hurry and he spoke between mouthfuls.

"James is on his way to Ogdensburg," he explained to Lucy.

"Oh my!" she said. "You are a long way off the road." Was he? Perhaps that explained why he hadn't been found yet, and why the MacKinnons had not heard of the escape. "Did you lose your way in the darkness?"

"I must have. I don't really know what happened. I wasn't feeling well, and I was very glad to find your barn."

"The hand of the Lord was guiding you," said Hugh, matter-of-factly. "Are you by any chance going to join the militia when you reach Ogdensburg?"

"I might. My friend, Jared – Malachi's boy – is a drummer, and I might join him."

"If you do, you will surely meet our boy Alex. He is in the militia there too."

"Is he? Has he…has he been in any fighting yet?"

"Not really. They were called to cross the river and capture a gunboat in the town over there – Prescott, is it? But they refused to go. As militia, they signed up to defend our country not to invade another, so they refused."

"Oh!" That was interesting. James wondered if Captain MacKessock was aware of it. "Do you think they were right in refusing?"

"Nothing is right about this war, but…I don't know. It seems to me, if you have to fight, you can't do it with half measures. It's a strange world we live in when you find yourself at war with your friends and neighbors."

"You have friends across the river?"

Hugh nodded. "And relatives. But I'm glad for Alex's sake there hasn't been much fighting. He only had to fire the big guns once. The British started to cross the river to capture our guns, I expect. But we drove them back. Some of their men were killed and one – just a boy I think, about your age – was washed up on our side and taken prisoner. He was in a bad way, poor lad, but your friends the Jacksons looked after him until he was well enough to go to prison."

"But I thought Malachi Jackson was in favor of the war …what they call a war hawk."

"That's true. It's a strange paradox of war that you do your best to kill your opponent, but if you only wound him, you do your best to help him survive. And of course, as a prisoner or maimed, he won't fight again." Hugh MacKinnon pushed an empty plate back. "Now, lad, are you sure you've had enough to eat? You have a long walk ahead of you."

"Oh yes. I can't thank you enough. But I must be on my way. If you would show me how to get back to the road…."

"Then here." Lucy MacKinnon handed him a package, wrapped in a piece of linen. "For the next time you are hungry. And if you meet our Alex, give him our love."

Their love! If I escape it will be more likely a musket ball, thought James. "I will," he said, hoping he didn't sound guilty. "You've been very kind. Perhaps I can repay you some day."

"You can repay us by helping someone else," said Hugh. "Now then, if you cross that field and go through those woods, you will see the road beyond the next pasture."

And so James set out – thankful for the food, thankful that the alarm had not yet been raised – in the direction that had been pointed out to him. But as soon as he was out of sight from the farm, he changed direction and headed back to the river. He had to find a boat, preferably a canoe, that would carry him back to his own side, back to Canada.

Sergeant Hare swung the boat close inshore. "Take a rest, lads. And have some more biscuits. We won't be able to roast our fowl or pork for a while."

"Should we not find the road and be after the boy, Sarge? He'll make good time on the road."

"Forget it. He won't go near the road. He'll be looking for a boat to get back to Canada. And he won't find one in the dark. My bet is he'll hole up somewhere for the night and scour the riverbank in the morning for a boat. All we have to do is make sure there's none available to him all the way back to Ogdensburg, just to be sure. Except one. I know just the place to leave a boat where he's sure to find it. As bait. When he goes for it, we'll grab him."

Chapter Twelve

There were no boats. Even where there were houses on the riverbank, even where there were jetties reaching out into the river, there were no boats. James couldn't understand it.

There *should* have been boats. Even though it was November and already there was ice forming in the bays and backwaters, even though the fishing season was long past, there should have been rowboats and canoes. They would have been tied up, perhaps; lifted out of the water for the coming winter – whatever. There should have been a boat there that he could steal.

He had trudged all morning, never far from the river. Sometimes he had to hide in ditches or behind bushes to avoid people – a farmer in the field, a housewife hanging out the wash. Sometimes he had to detour inland where a house was so close to the river that he could not pass. One such detour put him onto the road, where he came face to face with a woman who held a little boy by the hand. He saw a startled look come into her eyes, shaded by the deep brim of her bonnet. He had no doubt his own were equally startled. But he managed to touch his brow where the brim of his own hat would have been if he hadn't lost it, and wish the lady a pleasant good morning. She had nodded and smiled shyly, and the little boy had looked at him curiously as they passed.

"Who is that, Mama?" he heard the boy ask. He didn't hear the reply.

Was she wondering about him? Would she report the presence of a stranger in the area? Surely by now, news of his escape would be common knowledge. He *had* to find a boat. But there weren't any.

It must have been a little before noon, he guessed by the position of the sun, when he realized that he was approaching a village. He saw plumes of smoke rising above a grove of trees, and he heard dogs barking and the sound of a hammer ringing on iron – a blacksmith shop, no doubt.

A village. Here, surely, he would find a boat.

With renewed hope he approached along a snake rail fence through the grove to the farther fringe of trees. There was a mill, humming with activity, the big wheel turned ponderously by water spilling over a dam. Below the mill the stream rushed and deepened, sweeping over hidden stones toward the river, widening out into a placid pool. And there, on the far bank, where stream and river met, was a canoe!

He drew a long breath of relief. There was his means of escape, his transportation across the St. Lawrence to freedom.

But he must be patient. He knew that. He must wait until dark. Meantime he could make plans.

Over there, on the other side of the stream, was a dusty road leading down to the river shore. There were clapboard houses on either side, a small, whitewashed church, and the blacksmith's shop, where the smithy in leather apron was hammering an iron rim onto a wagon wheel, smoke and the smell of scorched wood hanging on the air. And down by the river, almost overhanging the lone canoe, was an inn. A wooden sign proclaimed it to be "The Dusty Miller."

The wind was rising, bringing with it pellets of icy rain. James hunched deeper into the collar of his coat. There was nothing he could do until dark. Thank goodness the November night came early. He thrust his hands in his pockets and felt the package Mrs. MacKinnon had given him. He opened it and found thick bread and cheese. He ate it, silently thanking the lady for her thoughtfulness.

There were some signs of life in the village as the afternoon wore on. The smith had vanished indoors. A man came down the road, leading a heavy draft horse into the smithy. He reappeared some time later, going back the way he had come. At one point children spilled out of one of the buildings that must have been a school and engaged in a game in the road that entailed much running and shouting and laughter before scattering in different directions. Women appeared, occasionally stopping to talk to each other and then strolling to another building that was evidently a store. Then, as the hidden sun sank lower, the road was deserted, and the tantalizing smell of food in preparation reached him.

Standing in the lengthening shadows, the collar of his coat turned up in a vain attempt to warm his ears, James could only wait and plan his next move.

The first challenge was to cross the stream. In summer he might have waded in, but now, with tattered boots and a long night ahead on open water in freezing temperatures, that was out of the question. There had to be a better way.

The mill, a tall four-storey building, was on his side of the water. He went upstream past it. But there was a wide, deep mill pond with no bridge in sight. That left just the dam itself, and to reach it, he would have to go through the mill.

He realized then that the sound of activity inside the mill had ceased. The work day was over. But he had seen no one emerge, either on his side of the stream or on the dam itself. The miller was still inside. James studied the situation from the shelter of a big oak. The miller would have to come out sooner or later, but when he did so, he would certainly lock the doors. With the gathering dusk it must be pretty dark inside, with shadows cast by the light from lanterns. If he could get in there, he might be able to avoid detection and slip out the other door onto the dam. He felt a growing anxiety in the pit of his stomach at the mere thought. But there was no alternative. There was no other way to reach that canoe.

He approached the door of the mill on silent feet and paused there, his ear against it. He could hear nothing.

He reached for the latch, realizing that his hands were trembling. He drew them back and clasped them together until the trembling ceased. Then he tried again, lifting the latch, pausing, listening. Nothing. He pulled the door open an inch then pressed an eye to the opening. There was only a faint, unsteady light inside. He could see no one. He opened the door a little further, ready to drop the latch and run, but there was nothing to indicate that his actions had been seen. He drew in a quick breath, opened the door wide enough, slipped inside and carefully shut it behind him.

He was aware of great beams reaching up into the darkness overhead, of shafts and conveyor belts and a line of rolling mills, all casting weird shadows created by the dim, flickering light of a few storm lanterns hanging here and there. He was also aware of voices – two men in conversation beyond the rolling mills. He edged forward to peer around them. The men were at the door – the door through which he would have to escape. Two men. If each went out a different door and locked it behind him, James would be trapped.

But there was no point in borrowing trouble. James pressed back into the shadows and waited.

They split up at last. One man pulled the door closed, and James was relieved to see that it was bolted on the inside. But the other man was approaching. James looked around anxiously. There were deep shadows between the rolling mills and a low partition. He squeezed in there, crouching, holding his breath.

And the man stopped. Right there. So close, James could hear his breathing. And he was looking directly his way. James closed his eyes lest their whiteness give him away, but he knew it was a futile gesture. His bulk couldn't be missed. He waited for the shout of discovery.

But perhaps the man wasn't sure what he was seeing, where there should have been nothing at all. He came even closer, the toe of his boot nudging James'. And James saw him through half-open eyes, reaching out a hand....

"Joe," the man called. And James knew that he was discovered. And yet there was no urgency in the man's voice. "Joe," he was saying in a normal tone, "remind me to replace the belt on number one mill in the morning. It's worn bad."

"Right, Caleb." And incredibly, the man called Caleb moved away.

James stayed where he was while his pounding heart slowed to a normal beat. Then he moved, carefully, silently, straightening cramped limbs. He looked around. There was no one in sight. There was no one near the door through which he had to escape. On the other hand, neither man had gone out the other door. They were both still there, somewhere. Where *were* they? They could be anywhere in this shadowy labyrinth. He listened until his ears ached, but he could hear nothing.

James edged alongside the rolling mills and paused in the shadow of a great beam that rose like the trunk of a gigantic tree. There was nothing between him and the door. Then he heard footsteps behind him. He moved around the beam. More footsteps from the other direction. In a moment he would be discovered. There was only one way to go. He darted across an open space, holding his breath, not daring to look back, and dropped down a set of stairs to the floor below.

Here were the great, wooden-cogged gears turned by the waterwheel, presently disengaged, dimly lit by a single storm lantern. He stopped, listening. The steps were coming nearer, following him, coming down the stairs.

There were deep shadows behind a low partition that closed off the mechanism. He climbed it and crouched there, his cheek hard against the greased rim of a cog wheel.

The man came on. Passed by. And reached up and blew out the lantern. The welcome darkness was relieved only by a dim light from the head of the stairs. The man climbed the stairs and was gone.

Carefully James followed him, feeling his way, tripping over some unseen object, catching himself, reaching the stairs.

One by one the lanterns were being extinguished. Then, as he stood with just his head above the floor, the last lantern went out and he heard the door closed. He was alone at last.

It was dark. Pitch dark. A window high up the wall was only a lighter shade of blackness. He climbed the stairs by feel. He knew the direction in which he had to go. He walked carefully, one foot tentatively ahead of the other, bumping into one of the grinding stones, going around it, reaching the wall, feeling his way along it, until at last he felt the hinges. He traced the shape of the door until he found the bolts. They slid back easily. The door opened. He stepped outside, pulling it closed behind him.

Below him the great wheel turned, the water splashing over the paddles, falling, to be whipped away in a ghostly white froth far below. And before him was the dam, a narrow, unfenced catwalk reaching to the far shore. On one side, the water was only inches below his feet; on the other, a deep drop into blackness. He didn't hesitate. He slipped to his hands and knees and crawled across to safety.

It was dark now, save for the soft glow of lamps in windows. His first thought was to go along the bank of the stream behind the houses, but there were picket fences right to the shore, and, in at least one yard, a dog with a deep, ominous bark. He would have to stick to the road.

It was suppertime. The road was empty. He passed the blacksmith shop, then the church. Ahead, at the end of the road, was the black bulk of the inn. Beyond and below it – somewhere in the darkness – was the canoe.

The door of the inn opened. A man appeared, outlined in the light. He came down the steps, closing the door behind him. James held his breath. The man was approaching, staggering a little, weaving from side to side. There was no way to avoid him.

He's drunk, thought James. Everyone knows everyone in a village like this. But maybe he's tipsy enough that he won't recognize me for a stranger.

The man was almost abreast before he saw James. He stopped, reaching out a hand. James' first impulse was to brush past and keep going. But no, that would be more suspicious than if he at least spoke.

"Good evening, George," he managed, keeping his face hidden in his collar.

"No no, you've got it wrong. Who d'you think I am? George Crow? Do I look like that fool? I'm Tom Benchly. Who are you? I can't see your face for your collar. Don't blame you though. It's a cold wind. Snow before morning. Going to the Dusty Miller, are you? You'll be warm there, though there's soldiers taking up the fire as if they own the place. I know you. You're Ben Hawkins, ain't you! Don't worry. If I meet your missus I won't tell her I seen you going to the Miller. And you won't tell Betsy, will you? Not that she won't know. Always knows when I've been to the Miller. I don't know how she cottons on every time, but that's women for you. Nose like bloodhounds."

"You're right." James was acutely aware that someone else was approaching. He had to get away. "Maybe you should go. You won't want to keep Betsy waiting." He edged away.

"Too true," said the man, with feeling. "I'll go. I see someone coming. I'll bet it's Ben Hawkins on his way to the Miller." He stopped, looking at James in a befuddled way. "But you're…no you ain't. Yes you are. I better warn Ben he's already here so he can go home before his supper gets cold. Mind what I say. Don't let them soldiers hog the fire."

James broke away with relief. He wanted to run now. The canoe was there, just beyond the inn. And if there were soldiers inside he must move fast before they came out….

Soldiers! He was aware of a growing uneasiness. Could the soldiers be Sergeant Hare and his men? James caught his breath at a sudden heart-stopping thought. Was it coincidence that there were soldiers here, right where the only canoe anywhere on the riverbank was his for the taking?

It must be a coincidence, he told himself. He wanted it to be a coincidence. There would be soldiers everywhere once his escape was known. All he had to do was get that canoe into the river and take off into the darkness. He could out-paddle any soldiers. There was no time to lose. With a shock he realized that he had stopped short, standing in the middle of the road. That would never do. He had to move.

He hurried into the darkness, stumbled over something, fell, saw the dark shape of the canoe just ahead of him, struggled to his knees…

A heavy hand fell on his shoulder.

And he knew, with bitter resignation, that it had been a trap.

Chapter Thirteen

"**A**re you hurt? Can I help you?"

It was no voice James could recognize. Certainly not the sergeant. And he couldn't imagine the others, his former captors, speaking in that concerned, gentle tone.

He looked up. This man was in no military uniform. He wore a tricorn hat that shadowed his face, a black frock coat and breeches above white stockings and buckle shoes.

"I saw you fall," he was saying. "I don't think I know you. You are a stranger to these parts?"

"Yes." The man wasn't one of the soldiers, but he was preventing James' escape none the less. How could James justify launching a canoe now, in the cold and darkness? For a moment he considered eluding the man and doing just that, but he knew it would be folly. The alarm would be raised and the soldiers were only feet away. He would have to bluff it out for the moment.

"I'm traveling to Ogdensburg," he said. But that wouldn't explain his presence here, in the shadows below the inn. "I was going to go in for a meal but I can't. I seem to have lost my purse. Thank you, but I will be on my way."

"To Ogdensburg! But, my dear fellow, you can't travel all night in this weather, especially with nothing to eat. I watched you from up the street. You're cold as well as hungry. I'll see you right, if you'll let me. I'm Simple – by name and perchance by nature as well – Josiah Simple, pastor to my flock at the Methodist Meeting House. Now, young sir, what is your name?"

"James–" he caught himself in time "–Scott. You're very kind but…"

"No buts." The voice was as firm as the grip on his arm. "Come, we'll go into the Dusty Miller since it's so close and–"

"No!" The soldiers! James tried to break away in sudden panic.

"Now now! Perchance you were brought up to swear off strong drink? Or are you averse to accepting charity? My dear fellow, we live by helping others. A cup of cold water to one in need, in Christ's name, is akin to serving Christ Himself. Come. I won't take no for an answer. The Dusty Miller serves excellent shepherd's pie, and a small beer will wash it down. Then we'll decide what's to be done with you."

The soldiers are more likely to decide what's to be done with me if we go in there, thought James. Desperately he hunted for some excuse to break away, but he could think of none. He felt himself propelled to the door of the inn.

There was only a dim light inside. Even so it took several seconds for his eyes to adjust. Then he caught his breath. There, on chairs by the fire, were Sergeant Hare and one of his men. What was his name? Brooke.

"Barkeeper?" the pastor called out cheerfully. "Oh, it's you, Cutler. Shepherd's pie for me and my friend, Mr. Scott. We'll take a table in the corner."

They'll recognize me for sure, thought James, burying his face in the collar of his coat. They'll recognize the coat. He stole a quick glance in the direction of the fire. He saw the sergeant look casually, briefly in his direction, then turn again to the fire. Perhaps, James thought, he won't suspect because I'm with Mr. Simple. Why doesn't *he* – the pastor – realize I'm the escaped prisoner? Surely he has heard by now….

Mr. Simple had taken his arm and led him to a table almost hidden between high-backed settles. James had a glimpse of a man in the neighboring booth and recognized another of Hare's men, Archer, sitting at the table. On the table were the remains of a meal, a bottle and a bell. A bell…?

James slid into his seat, holding his breath. There was only the back of the settle between him and Archer. Anything that was said would be overheard. He would have to keep talk to a minimum.

Why was Archer sitting there alone, with a bell of all things, on his table?

They were sitting by a window, a big window that stretched past both booths. Out there, just below them, was the canoe. James couldn't see it – he could see only the reflection of the interior behind them, with the forms of two soldiers by the flickering fire – but he knew it was there, just out of reach.

"So you're on your way to Ogdensburg? Do you have friends there?"

"I...no. No one. I understand there's a detachment of soldiers there. I'm going to join the militia."

What would Archer think of that? Then he realized with horror what such a statement might lead to. What if Archer decided to talk to him, one soldier to another prospective one? Or if Mr. Simple offered to introduce him to the sergeant?

"Mr. Simple," he said quickly, before anything else could happen, "what do you think of this war?"

"I'm against all war." Then the pastor shook his head. "No, I shouldn't say that. Maybe somewhere, someday, there will be a just war. But this isn't it. Whichever side claims victory, the only winner will be the devil. Young man, if you must join the army, that's your affair. But, by the very nature of war, you will meet many temptations to loose living and the abandonment of all the values to which I hope you have been raised. I will pray for you, James Scott. Not for your bodily welfare...though for that too...but for your immortal soul. And speaking of your bodily welfare, our shepherd's pie is coming if I mistake not."

It was undoubtedly good pie, rivaling his mother's. But James, acutely aware of the nearby soldiers, was in no position to appreciate it. He hunched back in the shadowed corner, still wearing his coat in spite of the warmth. It offered him some shelter from curious glances, and if he had to make a run for it in the cold night, he would need it for survival.

Thankfully Reverend Simple, who had removed his own coat, made no reference to it. He ate in satisfied silence, though occasionally casting thoughtful glances in James' direction. When he finished, he pushed back his plate and glass.

"Now, James," he said, "I have decided. You will stay the night with us – we have room aplenty. And tomorrow you can come with me to Ogdensburg. The chapel there is on my circuit. And I will introduce you to friends of mine–"

"Oh no!" James fought down a rising panic. "No, Mr. Simple. You're very kind but I can't put you to any more trouble."

Why had he said he was going to Ogdensburg? That was the last place he wanted to go. He had to find a boat long before he reached that town.

But Mr. Simple was going on. "Nonsense, my boy. What are Christians here for but to help others? You will have a good sleep in a warm bed, and in the morning we will go together to Ogdensburg and I will introduce you to my friends the Jacksons."

"The...the Jacksons?" James gulped. "You did say, the Jacksons?"

"That's right. Malachi Jackson. Don't worry. He's an important man but he's no snob. You'll feel at home with him and his family. He's promoting this war. I don't agree with him there. But if you're bent on joining the militia, he will welcome you with open arms. And he has a boy and girl about your own age. You will become friends, I'm sure."

"That…that would be grand," said James faintly. How would the Jacksons' react if this pastor suddenly appeared with James 'Scott', who was supposed to be in a prisoner-of-war camp? A hysterical laugh threatened to break out. He quelled it with an effort. Somehow he had to escape from this kindly man long before they reached Ogdensburg – supposing they managed to leave this inn without being stopped by the soldiers. He would soon know about *that* anyway. Mr. Simple was rising and putting on his coat.

It was then that the bell in the next booth rang.

The reaction to the sudden sound was astounding. Archer was on his feet, yelling. Sergeant Hare and Brooke sprang up, overturning their chairs, bumping into each other, stampeding toward the door. All three met there in a crush, sorted themselves out with angry curses, and disappeared out the door.

Rev. Simple watched all this in mild surprise. "My my," he murmured. "What was that all about?"

"I suppose I can tell you now." Cutler, the barkeeper, had come out to watch the proceedings, wiping his hands on an apron. "I was sworn to secrecy, but now that their plan has worked, it won't matter. You see, sir, the soldiers are after an escaped prisoner-of-war. They are convinced he will be looking for a boat to get back home across the river, so they have removed them all, all the way to Ogdensburg. All except one. That one out there. As bait. They used a line to rig it so that, as soon as someone touches the canoe, it will pull on a bell on that table behind you. That must be what happened. I'm glad it worked. The sergeant has been in a foul mood ever since they arrived. They have their man now, and they'll soon be gone."

"An escaped prisoner? Well, well." The pastor looked at James thoughtfully. "If I had known about that, I might have suspected you, my boy. But apparently I would have been wrong. Come, let us be on our way. Mr. Cutler, I will settle with you in the morning before we leave."

"I know you will, sir."

Come on! James wanted to run. Now. Before Sergeant Hare discovered his mistake. When he did, he would be in a worse mood than ever. James didn't want to have to go near the sergeant again. His luck could not last.

They left the inn together, agonizingly slowly. There were shouts and curses coming from the darkness where the canoe was. Mr. Simple seemed inclined to linger, but James walked on, as if unaware that the pastor was not at his side. Should he cut and run for it now, while he was still free? His feet were itching to go, almost dancing on the wet road. It was an effort to hold back. But he mustn't panic now.

"Come." Mr. Simple caught up to him at last. "We live beside the meeting house."

It was later. Much later. The night was wearing on. Sergeant Hare and Archer sat by the fire – Brooke at the table – staring at a bell that refused to ring again.

"We'll get him yet," growled the sergeant. "If Carson and Watt are doing their job, that canoe out there is the only means the boy has of getting home. There's nothing else for him between here and Ogdensburg."

"But what if he was out there somewhere in the dark and saw what happened…saw us at the canoe when the racoon, or whatever it was, tripped the line? He'll know it's a trap."

The sergeant shrugged. "As long as he's on this side of the river we'll get him."

Archer stirred restlessly. "We'd better get him soon or the army will be wondering where we are. Maybe we should let the public know there's an escaped prisoner on the loose."

"Not yet. You know what it would mean if it gets out that we let him escape. Demotion for me and the stockade for you."

"Maybe so, but we'll have a better chance of getting him again if the public is on the lookout for a stranger. There can't be that many strangers wandering around. Am I right, barkeeper?"

"You're quite right. The only stranger I've seen in many a month is the young lad that came in tonight with the parson. Never seen him before or heard of anyone by that name. James Scott, I think it was."

"James Scott? A young lad?" The sergeant and the private exchanged glances. "With the parson, you say. Yes, I noticed him. In a big coat, the collar pulled up hiding his face. A patched coat...you were in the booth next to where they sat, Archer. Did you see him?"

"No, couldn't see his face. Wasn't paying much attention. I heard the parson say he was going to keep him overnight and take him to Ogdensburg in the morning. That's all."

"And the parson...Simple, is it?...said he was a friend of his?" It was more a question than a statement. Sergeant Hare was looking at the barkeeper for an answer.

"Doesn't mean a thing," said Cutler. "Pastor Simple is a friend to every vagrant, hobo, down-and-outer, and every stranger, bless him."

Sergeant Hare was on his feet. "Archer, stay here. If that bell rings the two of you can handle it. I'm going to call on Reverend Simple."

"But it's past midnight."

But Sergeant Hare was gone.

A banging on the door roused Josiah Simple from a deep sleep. "What in the world...? Someone in trouble. Don't get up, dear. I'll see who it is."

"Nonsense. Whoever it is will be the better for a cup of tea."

"They'll be wanting more than a cup of tea by the sound of it. I'm coming," he called. "Patience! I'm coming."

He pulled on a robe and went to the door, his wife close behind him, holding a candle. "Who is it?" he called through the door. "Please make less noise. You'll waken our guest."

"Sergeant Hare. Open up, Mr. Simple. I must talk to you. It's urgent."

"Come in then. Just push. Our door is never locked."

The sergeant came in, brushing past the parson, looking around. "Your guest. Where is he?"

"My guest? I must protest, Sergeant. This is very high-handed of you. He is asleep, unless you wakened him with your noise, which would not surprise me. If you must, he's in there."

"Here?" The sergeant opened a door at the end of the passage and found himself looking at a neatly made, but very empty bed.

"He's not here. Hasn't been here. He's an escaped prisoner. You'd better not be holding out on me or it could go hard with you. Where have you put him?"

"I told you. In here. How was I to know he was an escaped prisoner…if you're right, which I doubt. I thought you caught your man when someone disturbed the canoe and made the bell ring."

"That? No. That was a dog or something. Come, Mr. Simple. Where is he?"

"We put him in here." Mrs. Simple was speaking quietly

but firmly. "If he's not there your racket wakened him and he fled."

"Oh, to be sure. Taking the time to make his bed first. This bed hasn't been slept in. How long since he retired?"

"Two hours or more. But we would have heard him if he'd come out here to the door."

The sergeant brushed past them and went to the window. It was closed, but opened to his touch.

"That's it. He went out the window. Hours ago." He swore.

"Please, Sergeant! Mind your language. There's a lady here."

"Oh. Sorry. This fellow. Where did you meet him?

"Down below the inn. You know, I never thought of it before, but if I hadn't stopped him I do believe he would have had a go at launching that canoe."

For a moment it looked as if the sergeant would explode with rage. He mastered himself with a visible effort, his lips forming an inaudible profanity. He turned to the door, paused a moment, then said through clenched teeth, "We'll get him yet. He *still* has to find a boat." And he was gone.

"Dear dear!" murmured Josiah Simple. "You know, at risk of being disloyal to my country, I almost hope the boy escapes."

James trudged through the night, his face buried in the collar against the snow, his hands deep in his pockets.

There was no point in staying near the river, since he now knew there were no boats anywhere on its banks. So he walked along the road. He was going to Ogdensburg after all.

He remembered where there was a canoe, out of reach of Sergeant Hare and his men.

Chapter Fourteen

Leah Jackson pulled the hood of her cloak about her dark hair and walked slowly toward the river. She still did this every Friday morning, though she knew that Jamie Shaw would not appear. He was in a prisoner-of-war camp, far away. What was that like, she wondered – bare boards for a bed, bread and water for food, bars and locks and guards to make sure he stayed there? And all the time he could have been here, in the Jackson home, enjoying all they could offer, including Leah's companionship. Or perhaps he would have been repatriated by now, safely at home and out of the war.

The war! What a mess it was making of their lives. Jared, as a drummer boy, was supposed to be exempt from actual fighting, but everyone knew the exemption meant nothing. Thank God there hadn't been any real fighting yet – except for that abortive attack by the enemy that had not only failed but had brought Jamie Shaw here, to be nursed back to health.... She smiled at the memory, then it was gone. For her father, that victory had been the one bright spot in the war. Since then, he had been angered by the seeming clumsiness of the American generals and the repeated failures to bring the war to a quick and victorious end. He was irked, too, by the attitude of the people of Ogdensburg, who couldn't be persuaded that their neighbors across the river were actually the enemy.

The river. There was ice forming around the reeds, spreading across the little bays, reaching tentative fingers out into the stream. Sooner or later, unless the winter turned out to be a mild one, it would be frozen over from one side to the other. What then? Would that make any difference if the water barrier was no longer there, dividing the two nations? She remembered last winter, going across on the ice with Jared and Pilot to meet Jamie half way....

Jamie! Everything reminded her of him. Jamie, who had chosen prison. Did he not care for her at all?

She turned sadly and began to walk toward the storage barn. Already the cutter had replaced the wheeled carriage, the latter having been stored here for the winter along with the canoe.

And then she saw the footprints. It was a moment before their significance dawned on her. There was only one set, coming across the field, going to the door, stopping there. And none going the other way. Someone was still inside.

Someone. A deserter, maybe, hiding out in fear? If so, he had picked the wrong place. Her father wouldn't hesitate to turn a deserter in, and the punishment was death. Her spirit rebelled at the thought. Her first brief inclination to call to her father evaporated. She would see for herself....

And then she noticed the other footprints – dog prints – going to the barn and back again. Pilot! But that didn't make sense. Pilot never hurt anyone, but he had never failed to announce the arrival of a stranger by barking long and furiously. Yet this time he had failed to do so.

The dog had been in his usual place when she had come out of the house, giving her a sleepy, one-eyed stare before burying his nose in his blanket again. Why had he not given the alarm?

There could be only one explanation. It had been someone Pilot recognized as a friend. But that was absurd. Friends didn't approach across a field and go into a barn without even calling at the house.

Intrigued rather than alarmed, Leah approached the barn cautiously. She noticed that the bolts had been drawn back, confirming that someone was still inside. She paused, one hand on the latch. What if?...but she pushed such questions aside. She threw the door wide open.

At first she could see only the shapes of the carriage, the canoe and a rack of garden tools. Whoever was there was back behind them, lurking in the shadows. She took a deep breath.

"Come out," she said, loudly and firmly. "I know you're in here. My father will be here in a minute."

There was a movement in the gloom, then a figure appeared, wrapped in a big, patched coat, the face hidden behind a high collar. He spoke.

"Leah!"

She gasped, staring, unbelieving. "Jamie!...Jamie, is that you?"

"Yes." He pulled the collar down. He stood there, momentarily struck dumb at the sight of her. Then he said, "Is your father really coming?"

"No. No, I just said that to scare...whoever it was in here." She shook her head in confusion. "Jamie, I don't understand. I thought you were in a prison far away from here."

"I escaped. I've been on the run for two days."

"Two days! Where...where have you been all that time?"

"Two very kind people helped me out. Of course they didn't know I was an enemy. One of them knew you. A Reverend Josiah Simple."

"Mr. Simple. Of course. He would help anyone in need." She was still in a daze. "Why?...what are you going to do?"

"I *was* going to stay in here until dark and then borrow your canoe and go home."

"You were going to stay here without even coming in to see me?"

"Not because I didn't want to. I've wanted to see you ever since I went to jail. To explain. But I could hardly come knocking on your door. I'm an escaped prisoner."

"No. Of course not. That was silly of me. But now…
what happens now?"

"That's up to you, Leah."

"Me? What do you mean?"

"You can call your father and turn me in. That's what
you should do."

"Turn you in! Jamie! How can you think that of me?
What do you take me for?"

"I take you for an American citizen, and I'm your
enemy."

"You're not an enemy!" She almost stamped her foot in
frustration. "You're a friend."

But he *was* an enemy. They both knew that. It was an
invisible barrier between them.

They were silent, acutely aware of each other's presence, wanting to break the barrier down, unable to do so.

"How did you know I was in here?" asked James at last,
his voice strained.

"Your footprints in the snow. Some coming, none
going."

"Oh. I never thought of that. I'm glad your father didn't
see them first."

"He's in his office. It's Friday morning. Did you know?
I still come to the river every Friday morning, even
though I know you won't come." She wasn't looking at
him. Her cheeks were pink, not just with the cold. "I'll get
a broom and brush over the footprints. Jamie…you said
you wanted to explain something."

"Yes. Why I chose to go to prison rather than stay with you. I *wanted* to stay. You have no idea how much I wanted that. But…" He told her then how Sergeant Hare and his men had mistreated the farmer and his wife. "Remember what the condition was? If I stayed, I had to promise never to take up arms against your people again. But what if I was at home and Sergeant Hare or someone like him came and did the same to my parents? I would have to stand by and do nothing. I couldn't do that. And my father is in the militia. I would have to let him do the fighting for me." He looked at her, wishing he could explain better. "Do you understand, Leah?"

But he wasn't to know if she understood or not.

"Leah!" Her father's strident voice carried clearly from the house. "Leah. Where are you? Your mother wants you."

"Coming father. I'll just be a minute."

She turned to James. For a moment they said nothing, still conscious of the barrier between them.

"I'll bring you something to eat," she said at last, softly. "When I have a chance. But I won't be able to stay. Be on the lookout. No one is likely to come this way, but you never know. Father would turn you in again. You know that. But I won't."

Another awkward moment, then she turned abruptly. "Good-bye, Jamie," she said over her shoulder. Then she was gone.

* * *

It was two days later. The Jackson family was still at the table, having just finished dinner. Malachi Jackson cleared his throat.

"I have news," he said, "that will be of interest to you. Your former friend, James Shaw, has escaped."

"No!" Jared's face lit up. He grinned. "He said he was going to try to get away, but I never thought he would pull it off. How did he manage it?"

"It would appear that Sergeant – rather, I should say, private – Hare made two mistakes. It was through his carelessness that the boy was able to slip his bonds and get away. Hare's second mistake was to cover it up, hoping to recapture James before the escape became known. As a result at least two people helped him out without knowing who or what he was. One was our own pastor, Josiah Simple."

"Mr. Simple! I'm sure he would have helped James anyway. How did the sergeant try to recapture him?"

"His plan was good," Malachi admitted grudgingly. "He guessed – correctly, I would say – that the boy would be looking for a boat to get back across the river. So he made sure no boats were available."

"Then James must still be on this side somewhere."

"I think not," said Mr. Jackson, gravely. "I rather think he has been successful in crossing the river. I was in the barn today. Your canoe, Jared, is missing."

"My canoe! You don't mean...you're right! He came here and he took it, right from under our noses."

"I'm afraid that's exactly what happened. Leah, what's the matter? Are you ill? You appear flushed."

"No father, I'm fine. Just a little warm."

"Leah." Jared looked at her suspiciously. "Did you hear what father said? James likely got away in our own canoe."

"Yes, I heard." She hesitated, then she looked around defiantly. "If he did, I'm glad."

There was a moment of electrified silence, then Jared said quietly, "So am I."

"He's a smart boy," acknowledged Mr. Jackson. He frowned, then shrugged. "It is the duty of every prisoner to try to escape. I hope you would do the same, Jared, if you should ever be captured. On the other hand it is everyone's duty to prevent the enemy's escape."

"I'm just glad," said Jared, "that he took the canoe instead of coming to me and asking for it. That would have been awkward."

"You would have done your duty," said his father severly. "You would have turned him in. We must all do our duty to our country. Surely my own family recognizes that those who may formerly have been friends are now enemies."

Leah and Jared looked at each other. "Yes, Father," they said.

Mrs. Jackson heaved a sigh and said nothing.

Chapter Fifteen

"This is a strange war we're fighting, Mr. Jackson. Or perhaps I should say, *not* fighting." Major Wilson turned from the window to address his visitor.

Malachi Jackson spread his hands in resignation and shrugged. "Not fighting is correct. Imagine! A war that grinds to a halt because it is too cold to fight. A war that should have been won by now if we had competent leadership."

"And a desire to fight. That, too has been lacking, Mr. Jackson."

"Around here, certainly. But desire isn't everything. Take the Kentuckians. A finer, braver body of men you'll never find anywhere, *and* they have a hatred of the British. When Henry Clay, our Speaker of the House, called for volunteers, more responded than could be handled. But they only signed up for six months, confident they would win the war well within that period of time.

When that didn't happen, they refused to sign up again. Of course they lacked two essentials: winter clothing and a good, solid military training and discipline."

The major nodded. "Well, when the ice breaks up we can start afresh with new leaders and lessons learned."

"True. I have just come from an extended trip to Washington, and I can tell you we have a new secretary of war and a growing optimism. But don't forget the enemy will also start afresh with new leaders and lessons learned. My guess is that there will be reinforcements from Britain just waiting for the ice to break up in the St. Lawrence. Your guns will be very important then, Major. We will still have numerical superiority, but they have seasoned, well trained troops."

"Yes. They're big on training and discipline, aren't they? I would call them parade square fanatics." He turned and opened the window. "Listen, Mr. Jackson."

Puzzled, Malachi listened for a moment, then a look of surprise crossed his face.

"Damnation! I know sound travels far over ice, but their sergeant-majors must have lungs of infinite capacity to be heard so distinctly all this way."

The major chuckled. "Not necessarily. Come and see."

Mr. Jackson joined him at the window. What he saw caused him to whistle in surprise. The river was frozen over from shore to shore, and out on the ice was what seemed, at least, to be a vast army – obviously a British army, dressed in long grey winter coats – marching and counter-marching, drilling, performing manoeuvres and formations, and all completely ignoring the fact that American cannons were a mere half-mile away.

"Good heavens! The audacity! How long has this been going on?"

"Oh, ever since the ice was solid enough to hold them."

"And you've done nothing about it?"

"I wouldn't say that. The first day or two we ignored them, but then, when they began to approach the half-way mark, we opened fire with a mortar or two just to let them know we're not asleep over here and they'd better not come any further. I imagine they saw the smoke from the guns because they scattered. I doubt we hit anyone. But we made our point. To fire any more would be a waste of powder and shot. Besides, they're not doing any harm and are affording our men considerable amusement, watching them perform manoeuvres that may have won them battles on the open fields of Europe but don't work here. Our men are beginning to realize how lucky they are to be in *our* army, where training and discipline are at least humane and sensible."

"Hmm. Maybe." Malachi Jackson sounded doubtful. "Perhaps a spell under Major-General Wade Hampton would convince them that we have our own disciplinarians. The guns appeared to be only partially manned when I came by."

"Oh? The captain must have found something more productive for them to do. Perhaps he's been inspired by our friends, the enemy, and has them out on the parade square. Might do them a world of good."

As a gust of icy wind blew inside, the major pulled the window closed.

"Incidentally, Mr. Jackson, you are aware, are you not, that our late prisoner who escaped, the boy your wife helped nurse back to health, made it all the way home?"

"I hadn't heard for certain, but I expected as much. In fact, major, I regret to say that we…my family…unwittingly aided in his escape."

The major was startled. "YOU did? What do you mean?

"I have every reason to believe that he stole our canoe to cross the river. Certainly it went missing just at that time. But without denying any responsibility, I must say that if Sergeant Hare had let it be known the boy had escaped, our canoe would have been locked up out of anyone's reach."

"Oh surely. You can't blame yourself. Sergeant Hare is utterly to blame for the whole sad affair. He's not a sergeant any more, of course. Now, Mr. Jackson, would you care to join me in a glass of brandy?"

"Thank you."

They were sitting at the officer's desk, sipping brandy, chatting idly, when something caused them both to stop short and look at each other with raised eyebrows. Then the major sprang up, upsetting his chair, and threw the window wide open.

"My God!" he gasped.

The redcoats were no longer scattered about in squads. They were in long lines, several deep, and they were running, running and shouting, charging across the ice, bayonets fixed. Charging toward the American guns.

"My God! They're coming."

Major Wilson swung round, collided with Mr. Jackson, flung him aside, threw open the door and disappeared, bellowing orders.

Malachi Jackson sprang to the window and groaned aloud. Yet another fatal error had been made. There would be no stopping that tide of men sweeping across the ice, led by swordbrandishing officers – even if the defenders had been prepared. And they were not.

"Where...where are our guns?" Mr. Jackson was sweating with anger and impatience. Then he heard the sound that must have been there earlier but was lost in the din – the urgent beating of a drum.

Good, he thought, with helpless pride. Jared, at least, was doing his duty.

At last the cannon came to life. They began to fire, at first with no visible effect. Then gaps appeared in that long line of insurgents, only to be filled up again immediately. A minute or two later and it was evident that at least one had been loaded with grape-shot. A swathe of redcoats fell like grain before a scythe. But there was no stopping that charge.

There was no time for either side to reload. It was a mad, screaming bayonet charge that could only end one way.

And, at that moment, Malachi Jackson heard the drumbeat cut off abruptly, in mid-roll.

He leaned heavily, helplessly against the wall, sickened by anger and chagrin at the utter defeat. And he prayed a wordless prayer for his boy.

James Shaw was part of that charge, caught up in the mad but disciplined rush. He was aware of the militia around him and of the regulars leading the way, all yelling something unintelligible. He saw the leading line pause to fire their muskets, then the next line following suit, and still no reply from the enemy. They must have been caught completely off guard. Then the cannon came to life, firing a ragged volley. Most of the balls rushed overhead to fall on the ice far behind. One or two cut an narrow alley through the lines, an alley immediately filled as if it had never existed. Something else, much more effective, hit that wall of men, scything through them so that men fell, dead and wounded. But again the gap was filled and James was carried forward in the rush, falling over a dead man, picking himself up and running, all the while listening for something else behind the yelling and the gunfire.

He heard it then, the steady, urgent beating of a drum, getting louder as he and his comrades bore down on the enemy. Then there was a sudden lull. James saw a white flag wave in the distance. For a brief moment the drumbeat continued. Then it was cut off, abruptly, in mid roll.

James knew the attack had succeeded, that the enemy had surrendered their guns. But there was no feeling of exultation. Only a growing anxiety for Jared.

Leah and her mother heard the shouting, the popping of musket gunfire, the delayed answering blast of cannon fire. They stood together on the stoop, wordless, wondering, fearing…listening for the beat of a drum. And one of them at least wondered, with a sense of dread, if Jamie Shaw was part of it all. And they too heard the drumbeat end abruptly. They could only stand and wait. And pray.

Jared Jackson stood to his post, closing his mind to the chaos around him, shutting out the roar of the guns, the shouts of the invaders, the cries of the wounded. The fear, rising in his throat – that must be conquered. The drum. Only that existed. His beat – the roll, the paradiddle, the flam, requiring nerveless hands to send its message – nothing else mattered. He was in a world of his own. He had to be. Or he would fail, let his comrades down. The swarm of invaders didn't exist….

But they did exist. An eternity passed in which he stood alone. But then at last his defences were breached. They were all around him. The drumsticks were snatched from his hands. A bayonet prodded him, urging him to move. The fear he had quelled rushed over him, weakening his knees, rising like bile in his throat, churning his stomach. Then was gone. Because he was alive and it was all over….

Chapter Sixteen

Colonel 'Red' George Macdonell, with the American Major Wilson by his side, faced the representatives of the town of Ogdensburg, crushed together in the meeting house.

"We have attained our objective," he said. "We have burned the fort and spiked the guns, rendering them useless, which was all we aimed for. But now we must decide what happens next. The men of the local detachment are now our prisoners, but frankly we don't want prisoners. We're not equipped to deal with them...though of course we will find a way if it is necessary to do so. We can do that and leave an occupation force here to keep the peace, but we don't want to do that either. The people of Ogdensburg and Prescott have been, and still are, friends and neighbors and even in many cases relatives. We want to keep it that way.

"Major Wilson tells me that he was instructed to cooperate fully with the town. With that in mind, what I propose is this: that we release our prisoners outright and retire back across the river, leaving no occupation force behind whatever. In return, I ask you to refuse to let the army repair or replace the guns. Unless their policy has changed, they will respect your wishes. In other words, relations between the two towns will return to normal, pre-war conditions, and the river will be open to any – and everyone."

One gray-haired, bushy-whiskered man stood and broke a moment's silence.

"As you know, Colonel, we have been aware of your proposal for several days and have had a chance to discuss it fully. We have agreed to accept your terms."

The colonel nodded in satisfaction. "Unanimously?"

"Almost, sir. Not quite. There was one notable exception."

"And I am that exception." Malachi Jackson stood up, his face red with anger. "I protest, and will continue to protest, any such agreement. We are in effect declaring ourselves neutral and in revolt against our own country. Our country is at war. Our men are dying at the hands of the enemy. To strike a separate peace with them is to turn our backs on our own men. To promise to leave the river open is to stab our own men in the back, because it will be open only to our enemy, and his reinforcements and supplies. To visit and trade with the enemy is to deny the authority of our elected representatives, to deny the very democracy our fathers fought and died for."

"But Malachi, what is the alternative? They are going to control the river here anyway…either this way or by force. Are we to live with an occupation army in our midst that will restrict our freedom and keep the river open anyway? There is only a mile or two of river in question. If our army considers it important, they can bring in more guns and place them five miles upriver or five miles downriver as they choose. You use fine words, Malachi, but you are not facing the reality of the situation. By a big majority, Colonel, we are pleased to accept your terms."

"Maybe you are, but I am not." Malachi Jackson pushed his way to the door, paused there and looked back, scorn on his face. "Let it be known," he growled, "that the Jackson family at least is still at war, and no enemy will be welcome in our home until the war is officially over and the victory won." He stormed out.

* * *

A cold, blustery wind blew along the open plain of the river, lifting the loose snow from the ice, piling it along the bank, and whipping it into swirling mists that moved at its whim like angry ghosts.

Leah Jackson pulled the hood closer about her head and looked listlessly out over the river. It was Friday, but Jamie wouldn't come. She knew that. Her father's refusal to recognize the truce between the two towns was well known on both sides of the river. Already people had been visiting back and forth. Perhaps Jamie had come over too, but he would know enough not to approach the Jacksons' home....

She turned and started back toward the house. Her mother would guess where Leah had been, but would say nothing, silently sympathizing as they ate breakfast. Her father would be too preoccupied with his own thoughts to notice the comings and goings – and the mood – of his daughter. It would be a silent meal, each of them aware of the empty chair that was Jared's.

"Leah!"

She stopped short, her heart leaping. It was a low voice, not much more than a whisper, and she knew who it was. She looked fearfully toward the house, then to the barn, and she saw him standing at the corner out of sight of the house.

"Jamie! You shouldn't have come!" But she couldn't keep the gladness out of her voice.

"I know," he said. "I'll only stay a minute. But I had to see you, Leah. To let you know..." To let her know what? That he loved her? He couldn't say that. "...to ask about Jared. Is he all right?"

"Yes. He's with the army at Sackets Harbor. We hear from him now and then. There's a lot of sickness at the base. It must be horrible. But he's fine. And you...are you still with the militia?"

"Yes, but I won't be called on to fight unless your army comes back and invades nearby. And I hope they won't do that. I came over to Ogdensburg once since the truce. I looked for you but didn't really expect to see you. Have you been to town?"

"Once or twice. But only with father. If I did see you… I wouldn't have recognized you. I'm sorry about his…his stubbornness. But it means we can't meet any more. You understand?"

"Yes, I understand. But the war can't last forever. Can I come again when it's all over?"

"Of course. I come to the river every Friday, even though I know you won't be there…and someday you will be."

Someday. Someday the barrier that was between them would be gone forever.

He reached out a hand. For a moment hers was in his clasp, warm and lingering, leaving a message that thrilled him. Then they both turned and went reluctantly in opposite directions.

Chapter Seventeen

The long summer passed, and everything was quiet in the Ogdensburg and Prescott areas, but news came through of American victories in the west. Malachi Jackson was enthusiastic.

"At last," he said, "we're going to do what should have been done months ago. We're going to cut the enemy's supply lines." He pushed back his plate, looking at his wife and daughter with satisfaction. "Finally we have had some good news this past summer. Commodore Perry has control of Lake Erie, so we've retaken Detroit and now occupy the west country. True, we're still at a halt in the Niagara area, thanks to more blunders, but we can solve that problem and bring this war to a victorious conclusion by taking Montreal. And that, my dears, is what we should have done long ago."

"Montreal?" Mrs. Jackson sounded relieved. "Then surely Jared will not be involved. Montreal is a long way from Sackets Harbor."

"No no, you have it wrong. There will be a force attacking Montreal from Plattsburg, and that should suffice, for to my knowledge there is no fort at Montreal. But we are taking no chances. A big army is being assembled at Sackets Harbor and will be moving downriver soon to attack from the west. It may already have started." He looked uneasily to where a mixture of rain and sleet lashed against the window. "Or will, once the weather cooperates."

"Downriver?" Leah's face was pale. "Then they will be going right past us out there. Won't the guns at Prescott stop them?"

"No. We will have to keep close inshore and slip by in the night. It will be slow going, more or less in single file, for there will be many boats. We may lose a few, but it can be done." He frowned. "It will mean more delay, and we can't afford that, but it can be done."

"But the river is shallow close to shore. Too shallow to allow heavy boats to pass, isn't it?"

"Good for you, girl. You see the problem. You are right. The men are going to have to get out and walk, then the supplies and ammunition will have to be reloaded so no boat is too heavily laden. And all that will take time...time we can't spare. The army will have to march and keep pace."

Leah was picking at her food, not looking up. "On this side of the river? Or the other?"

"I expect on this side until they are past the threat of the Prescott guns. Eventually of course they will have to cross over. They can't go much further by boat because of the rapids."

"Then" she said, softly, "the Canadian militia will be involved."

"Oh, undoubtedly," agreed her father. Then he looked at his daughter. "You will be thinking of your former friend, James Shaw?"

She nodded. "Yes, Father."

He shrugged. "Too bad he escaped. He would be safe in a prison camp otherwise."

He looked again to the window and some of his enthusiasm evaporated. "Why?" he muttered. "Why have they waited so long? Surely the need was apparent months ago. Now we've left ourselves no leeway. Winter will soon put a stop to everything again. It's just one delay after another, and then those infernal guns of Prescott..."

He stopped short. There was a faraway look on his face. He tapped his fork absently on the table. "By heaven! I wonder..."

"You wonder...what, dear?" asked Mrs. Jackson.

"Did I ever tell you," he said slowly, "of a plan we once formulated to capture a gunboat from the British? No? Well, it was in Prescott, and we figured out how to take it. A small force led by our Jared would go up stream by night, land..." he looked at Leah, "at your friends the Shaws' place, and surprise the garrison there by attacking from the rear."

"Led by *Jared*! But Malachi, he's only a boy."

"Yes he is, but he knows every step of the way between the Shaws and Prescott better than anyone...except maybe you, Leah. You two, with the Shaw boy, explored that country, didn't you? Then, you see, while Jared's force distracts the redcoats, another force would cross directly and take the gunboat."

"But Malachi, what do you mean when you say 'we'? You are not a soldier. And surely you would not go along with a plan that would put your own son in such danger."

"Our son, my dear, *is* a soldier and must obey orders. It was Major Wilson's plan, but I agreed to it because it was a good plan and Jared could use his knowledge for his country. As it turned out, it was never put into practice, but it would have worked then and it would work now." His enthusiasm was returning. "A small force, landing at the Shaws' and attacking the guns from the rear would give our flotilla time to pass in midstream, and save at least a day."

"With Jared guiding them again?" Mrs. Jackson's voice trembled. "Surely it would be suicide. The British must have a good-sized army at Prescott by now."

"As a matter of fact, they have not. Some of them were sent to Kingston, others to Montreal, because they didn't know which one would be our target. The men who stayed behind are scattered all along the river. They don't know where we will be landing. The main body will undoubtedly be coming from Kingston now that they know we are headed for Montreal, but they will not arrive for some time and the guns are vulnerable." He smiled. "As you know, I was against the truce that opened up the river between us and Prescott, but it has proved valuable. Our spies have been able to determine the strength and disposition of the British troops…knowledge which I am sure General Wilkinson does not have. I must go to him with it now."

"He's just a boy," Mrs. Jackson whispered.

"I'm sorry, dear. I am as concerned for Jared as you are, but I must do my duty and so must he. And so must we all. I will take our swiftest horse and leave within the hour. This could mean the difference between winning the war this year and having it wear on for at least one more." He hesitated, looking at his wife and daughter. "Do you understand?"

They both hesitated, then nodded reluctantly.

Leah understood – understood that if the plan was acted upon, her worst fears would soon be realized.

* * *

Captain MacKessock looked at the Canadian Militia drawn up before him.

"Men," he said, "I have news, a proclamation, and a challenge to present to you. First, the news. The American army is planning to capture Montreal. I don't need to emphasize the seriousness of the situation in which our country would be placed, should they succeed. They must not succeed.

"They have planned a two-pronged attack. One army already moved north from Plattsburg along the valley of the Chateauguay River. As you know, Colonel Macdonell was dispatched a little while ago to Montreal with a small detachment of select militia. We have just had word that he, along with French and Indian allies, has ambushed the American army and sent them packing back across the border. We need not worry about them again at least until spring."

A lusty cheer broke out from the ranks before him. He paused, then held up his hand for silence.

"The threat, of course, is far from over. A vast army is already on the move from Sackets Harbor down the St. Lawrence. In that respect, I have here a proclamation from the commanding officer of their army to be read to you. It goes thus: "'To the good people of Canada West living in the St. Lawrence River valley...'" He paused, looking up from the paper in his hand. "You will note that this is addressed only to the good people. The rest of you need not listen." Laughter. He returned to the paper. "'To the good etcetera etcetera. The army of the United States of America has no quarrel with you and wishes you no harm. If you remain at home and do not take up arms in an effort to delay our advance down the river, we promise to protect your persons and property now and in the future.'" His voice was drowned out in laughter. He paused, letting it go on for a few moments, then he spoke again, refusing to smile.

"Men, I'm serious. If any of you want to take advantage of this offer, you are free to do so, and your decision will be understood and respected. You can fall out now." No one moved. The captain smiled.

"Just as I expected. Now for the challenge. You are trained as skirmishers. Now you can put your training to good use. I want you to harass and annoy and pester the enemy in any way you can. Whenever their boats come within range, I expect them to be subjected to musket fire from behind the trees where you will be following their advance. You may not do much actual harm except to their morale, but that is vastly important. I expect they will go ashore on the other side to avoid our guns at Prescott, but eventually they will have to invade our country on foot to avoid the rapids. I want you to be there, harassing them from all sides without actually being drawn into a pitched battle. Meantime, reinforcements are coming from Kingston. When they arrive we will chase the Americans, watching for a site that will give us an advantage. When we find it, and the time is right, we will force them into a battle that will decide the fate of Montreal."

He paused again, to let his words sink in. "That is all. Your officers will advise you. Follow their orders. Our allies in Lower Canada won a great victory against overwhelming odds at Chateauguay. We will not let them down."

James Shaw listened with mixed emotions: excitement at the prospect of action; thankfulness that he was not shackled by a promise not to fight; and concern. The army was coming from Sackets Harbor. Jared Jackson would be one of them. Please God he would be unharmed....

***

The American flotilla suffered delay after delay. Fever and dysentery swept the camp, affecting even the general himself. Then an early winter storm with lashing winds and mountainous waves overturned boats and scattered provisions. Finally the armada, at harbor overnight, was hemmed in for a day by a hit-and-run raid by British gunboats.

At last, with the warm sun of Indian summer giving the autumn leaves an irridescent glow, the flotilla moved downriver with flags flying and fifes playing.

Snipers fired at them from the trees bordering the river. British gunboats, snapping at the heels like terriers, lobbed cannonballs into their midst. These were nuisances that could be endured. The invading army was finally underway.

But General Wilkinson knew that the guns at Prescott would mean more hindrance and Indian summer could not last much longer. At this point he was ready to listen to any scheme that might prevent any further delay.

Chapter Eighteen

What was she to do?

Leah stared unseeing out the window where the last leaves of autumn were drifting down to spread a red and gold carpet over the lawn. If her father's plan was to be put into motion – and she was sure it would be – then Jared would be at the head of a force crossing onto Canadian soil, right at the Shaws' homestead. Jared and James would almost surely come face to face. And each would have to try to kill the other.

She must prevent that at all costs. No one else could. But how?

She could cross over to the Canadian shore by canoe – the open water policy meant that there would be no problem. And she could warn the Shaws that their enemy was coming. But what would *they* do? They would be duty bound to warn the garrison at Prescott, and an ambush would be laid for the invaders. Then she would be betraying her own country. Her own brother. She could not do that.

What was the alternative?

If only she could lure James over to her side, to keep him there until the danger was past. He would come if he thought she needed him. She was sure of that. But how was she to go about such a scheme? How to get word to him? She knew of no one she could entrust with such a message. There had to be another way.

Her father was gone, to take his message to General Wilkinson – he'd been gone for two days. The flotilla must be well on its way downriver. If his plan was to be acted upon, it would be very soon. She had to do something now. Tonight.

She sat on the bed – the bed in which James had recuperated almost a year ago – and began to form a plan that would depend on careful timing if it was to succeed. She would cross the river in the darkness and conceal herself on the Canadian shore. She knew just the place – a grove of trees on the edge of the Shaws' property. And she would wait there until she was sure the Americans were coming…wait, in fact, until they were almost there.

Then she would run and warn the Shaws. That would give the family time to get away without having time to spread the alarm. The thought occurred to her that Thomas and James might not leave, but might stay and fight, even if the odds were two against…fifty? She dismissed it. She would have to persuade them to think of Rachel and Mary, not to be heroic.

It was a crazy scheme. If she was caught she would be

branded a traitor. But she was desperate.

After the evening meal, Leah excused herself on the pretext of having a headache. At dusk she let herself out the back door, ran silently to the shed, and dragged the canoe – a replacement for the one James had borrowed – to the river. She launched it and began paddling. She was wrapped in her dark cloak, with bread and cheese in the pocket, for she knew she might have a long, cold wait.

What if the force did not come tonight? Could she hide out for a whole day on the very edge of the Shaws' homestead without being discovered? Could she stay away from home that long? Her mother would be frantic.

No. It had to be tonight. She refused to consider anything else.

She passed the Ogdensburg waterfront. No one challenged her. The town was very quiet, as if waiting nervously for a storm to break. Across the river, in the gathering gloom, she could see the shapes of the guns. Guns that were waiting for the flotilla that they must know was coming. Guns that would be silenced if Malachi's plan was successful....

She paddled on. She knew both sides of the river. She passed the place where, in the cold dawn, she had waited to warn James once before. Across the river trees grew to the water's edge. There could be lookouts there, watching for the American boats to appear. She stopped paddling, drew into the shore, and waited there, until only the stars shone far overhead and the world was wrapped in darkness.

At last she set out again, until she was opposite the Shaws' homestead. Then she crossed the river, paddling fast, bumped the shore, sprang out and pulled the canoe clear of the water. The Shaws' home – set back below a line of trees – was in darkness. That was what she expected. They would be in bed, asleep. She was relieved they were. It would be that much easier to remain concealed until the time came to act.

She pulled the canoe into the grove, sat beneath the trees on the very edge of the river, and waited.

Was she doing the right thing? The question haunted her until she made a conscious effort to shut it from her mind. She was committed now. She had to go through with it. It *would* work....

The sound came at last, the gentle whispering of boats pushing through the still water. She peered into the darkness until she made out the white feathery waves at the bows, and the tall masts and billowing sails etched against the stars.

She wanted to run then, to warn the Shaws. But she had to be certain. She waited, breathless, until she knew beyond all doubt that two boats were turning into shore. Then she turned and ran.

She tripped and fell headlong. She hurt her knee, twisted her ankle. Her foot was caught. Pain shot through her. She smothered a sob, tried to get up. For a moment she couldn't move. Fearfully she looked back over her shoulder. She saw the snub nose of the first boat bunting the shore, the figure of a man in the bow. In a moment, as many as a hundred men would be swarming ashore. Desperately she yanked her foot free of whatever was holding it, ignoring the pain. She was on her feet. Her ankle gave, throwing her down again. But she had to get up, to get to the Shaws' house.

They were coming. Was that Jared in the lead? She dare not let them find her here on enemy soil. She would never be able to explain.

She was up, hobbling, lurching toward the house.

A shout behind her. She had been seen. She had left it too late. No, she hadn't. There was still time if she could rouse the Shaws. They could still get away.

She reached the house, and limped around to the back door, where she would not be seen by the American soldiers.

She beat on the door with her fists, called out, called out again between sobs. But there was no answer.

Her countrymen were coming. They must have heard her. It was too late. All her efforts had been for nothing. Jamie and his parents were trapped. She could only save herself. She turned and ran into the blackness of the trees. She collapsed in a heap, suddenly numb and drained.

As if from far away, she heard the soldiers come to the house, bang on the door. She heard shouts, the sound of breaking glass. Then a voice came clearly. "There's no one here. They've pulled out."

No one there! All her mad efforts, and the Shaws weren't even at home! Of course not. Jamie and his father would be away – probably at Prescott – with the militia. And Mrs. Shaw would have taken Mary away to safety, away from the river. Why, oh why hadn't she thought of that before she ever left home?

It had all been for nothing! She began to laugh hysterically, a laugh that she managed to smother before it dissolved into tears of pain.

She heard a voice call out "There's someone here. I swear I saw someone running toward the house."

"All the more reason why we should get going, before she raises the alarm." That was Jared. And he had said *she*. Had he recognized her? Had he guessed...?

She didn't know. She was past caring. She huddled in the darkness in a sea of pain, only half aware that the soldiers had landed and had gone off in the direction of Prescott.

Then, slowly, the realization came to her that now was the time to escape, to get back home before her absence was discovered. Fighting back tears, Leah hobbled out from the shadows that concealed her, out to the front of the house. Then she stopped short in dismay. The boats were still there. The crews were still there. She could see them, on the shore, in the bows. There was no way she could avoid being seen if she tried to launch the canoe. She was trapped.

Chapter Nineteen

The rattle of musket fire from the direction of Prescott shattered the quiet of the night – several shots, a momentary lull, then a fusillade punctuated by the sharp blast of a carronade.

Leah huddled in the deep shadows below the house and listened numbly. Jared would be part of that barrage. And maybe Jamie too. And she was helpless and a long way from home.

The din continued for some time, then ceased abruptly. For what seemed like ages, an eerie silence prevailed. Then came the sound of running feet, and men began to appear out of the forest. Some were running freely, some limping. Some were helping wounded comrades.

She heard them shouting to the waiting crews.

"No good. Too many of them. They held us off."

A voice of authority called out bitterly, "Signal the general. We failed."

Still they were coming. Leah watched – her face hidden in the collar of her cloak – watching for Jared, listening for some word of him.

"Many casualties?"

"Some. A few killed and some too badly wounded to run for it. The rest scattered."

"Are you being chased?"

"Don't think so. The redcoats know our army is coming. They can't leave the guns. Or they smell a trap."

The voice of authority spoke again. "We can't wait any longer. Two more minutes, then we shove off and rejoin the army."

"What about the rest?"

"They'll have to look out for themselves. They know what to do."

Two more minutes! And Jared had not returned. In spite of the darkness, she was sure of that. He must be either one of the casualties or had scattered with the others.

She waited, anxious, helpless, as the men climbed aboard and the boats pushed back into the stream. Two more men came, one limping, the other helping him. They saw the stretch of water between land and boat widening and they called out, but there was no response. Then one of them saw Leah's canoe, half hidden in the grove.

"Here we go, Luke. Hang on, we'll make it yet." And they pushed the canoe into the river and paddled away after the boats.

Her last means of escape was gone. But she didn't care. She had to find Jared.

She tore a long piece of cloth from her petticoat and bound her swollen ankle as tightly as she dared. She stood up, testing it tentatively. It felt better, but she would have to go slowly, favoring it.

She found the path that she, Jamie and Jared had used to go to Prescott many times. It was rough, in places not clearly marked, here and there overgrown. But she knew it well enough that it didn't matter.

She hadn't gone far when she met an American soldier limping toward her.

"You're too late," she said, unsteadily. "The boats have gone."

He stared at her in amazement. Then he cursed softly, and turned away. She caught his arm.

"Do you know Jared Jackson? I'm looking for him. He's a drummer. He was leading you…"

"Jackson? Yes, I know him. No idea what happened to him. Who are you?"

"I'm…" She caught herself. "I'm a friend. I must find him."

"A queer war," muttered the other, "when enemies are friends. He's either dead, or wounded, or obeying orders to disperse and catch up with the army later…which is what I'm going to have to do now."

"Oh. How will you do that?"

"Wait till daylight, for a start. Then circle round the town…*way* around. No one's going to help me…*that* I can be certain of. Then rejoin the army when it lands beyond Prescott. Right now I'll go back to where we landed until it's light enough to see where I'm going. There was a house there. There'll be a bed, and maybe some food...." He peered closely into her face, obviously wondering what a young girl was doing there, then he shrugged and moved away.

She went on. If Jared was dead or wounded, she would surely find him at the fort. If he wasn't there, he too must be obeying the order to rejoin the army. He would have no problem finding his way even in the darkness.

A few minutes later the guns at Prescott opened fire.

No rattle of muskets this time, but the overwhelming roar and blast of twenty-four pounders hurling balls of iron and shells of jagged steel into the sky. Flames from their muzzles lit the sky like an angry dawn.

She covered her ears, hurting even at that distance, and hobbled on.

She came at last to the town. The din was almost unbearable. In spite of that, there were people standing about, ears covered, staring across the river. Fires had started over there, and in the glow, a line of boats could be seen moving slowly but surely, hugging the far shore. In spite of the barrage, in spite of the fact that gaps appeared suddenly, the line kept moving. There was no stopping it. And it was obvious that the boats held supplies only. The army itself was on foot, encircling Ogdensburg, out of range of the guns.

Leah limped through the town. No one noticed her. They were too intent on the drama playing out before them. She approached the fort. Where would the dead and wounded be? Casualties from both sides would be under a doctor's care. In the fort? Probably. How would she get in there? She circled around, away from the riverfront. There was a gateway through the palisades, and beyond that, the main door was protected by a carronade. And a sentry on duty. She approached him hesitantly.

"Here, miss, where are you going?"

"I hoped…" She faltered. "…I wondered if a friend of mine had been wounded. James Shaw of the militia. And I thought maybe I could help care for the men that have been hurt."

"James Shaw? Would that be Thomas and Rachel's boy? You're in luck. His mother's here. Just you wait a minute." He turned and called to a sentry at the inner door, "Dave, ask Mrs. Shaw to come here for a minute, will you? She's got a visitor."

Rachel Shaw! For a moment Leah wanted to turn and run. How would Jamie's mother react, knowing that Leah was an 'enemy', that a few minutes ago her countrymen had been here, intent on killing and conquering? But Leah couldn't have run anymore if her life depended on it. She leaned helplessly against the palisade, easing her ankle, and waited.

"Leah? Leah Jackson!" Rachel Shaw stared in amazement. "What in the world…" Then she noticed Leah's pain-filled, exhausted face, and she opened her arms. "My dear! What has happened? You are hurt, aren't you." She turned to the sentry. "She's a friend of mine, and we can use her help. Will you let her in with me?"

"If you say so, ma'am."

"Come, Leah." She put her arm around the girl, supporting her. "It's your ankle? Come in here and sit. I can spare a few minutes. I'm helping the doctor with the wounded. And you can tell me how you come to be here, of all places."

"Thank...thank you." Leah fought back tears of gratitude. "It's Jared. I don't know what happened to him. And Jamie. I was afraid they would meet and...is Jared one of the wounded, Mrs. Shaw? Or...dead?"

She gazed at the girl in awe. "So that's it! Leah! You came all this way. No, my dear, Jared is not here. We've brought in all the bodies and wounded. If he was with them, he got away. You don't need to worry about your brother. He's safe."

"Oh. Thank God. And...and Jamie?"

"Jamie and his father aren't here. They're away with the militia, I don't know where. Were you...?" She looked at the girl's pale face, her dark, haunted eyes. "Were you worried about him too?"

Leah nodded, wordlessly.

For a moment Rachel said nothing, holding Leah in a close embrace. "They're two very fortunate boys," she whispered then, "to have such a brave and devoted friend and sister. I don't know what you've been through, Leah. You can explain, if you like, when we have time. But right now I must go and help the doctor. And Leah, I need your help. We have wounded from both sides. You can bathe faces and cool brows and wash wounds without doing any further damage to your ankle. Would you do that?"

"Oh yes, Mrs. Shaw. Please let me. Anything...."

Chapter Twenty

Rachel Shaw sat on a canvas chair, her legs stretched out before her, her head thrown back, resting against the wall behind her. There were streaks of dirt on her face and encrusted blood on her dress. Her eyes were closed. Leah lay curled up on a makeshift cot, breathing deeply. Her frock too was soiled, her eyes closed.

That was how Captain MacKessock found them – in a small room off the temporary hospital, dimly lit by a single lamp.

He was about to back out again silently, but Mrs. Shaw opened her eyes.

"You wished to speak to us, Captain?"

"Yes." He closed the door gently behind him. "I don't want to disturb you. You've earned a long rest. I just want to thank you for what you have done here tonight. The doctor and the wounded are very grateful. A woman's touch makes all the difference."

"I'm glad we were able to help. They are so young. And some are badly hurt."

"Yes. And this young girl." He looked at Leah. "She did a fine job, the doctor says. I don't recognize her. Does she live in Prescott?"

Rachel smiled. "No. She's from Ogdensburg."

"Ogdensburg! You mean she's…she's the enemy?"

"No, Captain. She's a friend. The very best of friends."

Captain MacKessock sighed. "As many of us have said before, this is a strange war. What will you do now, Mrs. Shaw? Return to your home?"

"No, not yet. Not as long as the threat from the river exists. Mary is with her grandmama, and Thomas and James are both somewhere with the militia. So I will stay with friends in town."

The captain hesitated, then said awkwardly, "Mrs. Shaw, I have a favor to ask of you."

"Oh?" Her interest quickened. "What can we do for you, Captain?"

"There is another battle coming. There has to be. We must stop the Americans before they reach Montreal, or our country is doomed. They bypassed Ogdensburg and are back on the river. Our militia and the Indians are harrassing and delaying them all along the riverbank to slow them down and give our army from Kingston a chance to catch up. They will have to land to go around the Long Sault Rapids. That's where we hope to catch up to them and force a showdown. It will be a desperate effort. As usual we will be badly outnumbered. But Colonel Morrison's troops are seasoned veterans, and if he can choose a site to his liking, we have a chance. But of course it will mean casualties. On both sides. That can't be avoided. And that's where we could use your help. Yours and the young girl's. And any other ladies you may be able to recruit."

"Of course, Captain. I will be glad to come. But Leah...she must get home to Ogdensburg. Her mother doesn't know where she is and must be terribly worried."

"She doesn't know?" Captain MacKessock's curiosity was evident, but he quelled it. "I'm afraid it will be impossible for anyone to cross the river for at least a day or two. The people over there are not happy with us just now. Our guns were set too high when we began our barrage last night, and some of our rounds damaged a number of their buildings. But I have ways and means of getting a message across. If you give me the name of her parents, I will see that they are informed."

"That would be a weight off our minds. Her name is Leah. Her father is Malachi Jackson."

"Malachi Jackson! Of course! Your families have been friends for years, haven't you? And it was the Jacksons who nursed your James back to health when we failed to take their guns and he was captured."

"Yes, Captain. That was mostly Leah's doing. We're very grateful to her. I don't know if...."

Mrs. Shaw stopped. Leah had stirred and opened sleepy eyes. "I think I heard what you were saying," she said. "There is another battle coming, and there will be more wounded who need our help. If you can really get word to Mother, then I would like to come with you."

"But, dear, your ankle." She turned to the captain. "She has a sprained ankle. She should keep off it. It would mean a long march, would it not?"

"Oh no, I would not ask that of you. We will see that you have a place on a gunboat, or maybe even the colonel's gig. And you will be kept safe until the battle is over and you are needed."

"Mrs. Shaw," said Leah, "if you are going, I want to go too."

Rachel hesitated only a moment, then nodded.

"You arrange it, Captain. Yes, we will come."

Chapter Twenty-One

The brief glow of Indian summer faded and died. The wind turned cold, bringing with it intermittent rain, sometimes laced with sleet.

James Shaw stood behind a tree as dusk gathered, and watched the long line of American boats go by. Some were under sail, some propelled by long oars known as sweeps. Now and then James fired his musket in their general direction, not knowing if he hit anything, hampered by the need to preserve ammunition. Further on, other lone men were doing the same thing, and from a point downriver, a small cannon belched smoke and flame. That at least had some effect. One boat was hit, swung around out of line, causing a confused pileup.

Then from upriver, in the direction of Prescott, he saw a sudden flame leap into the sky and heard the sound of gunfire, and he knew that he would not be able to hold position much longer. The enemy had sent a force ashore to clear the banks of such nuisances as himself.

As he watched, James saw more flames. The invaders must be burning the settlers' houses. Nothing else would account for that volume of smoke and flame, he thought. James and a few other militia men and Indians had stayed in such a house for the past two nights with the owner, one Alexander Craig, whose wife and children had been evacuated to a safer place. Would his house be the next to go? James turned and ran.

Alexander Craig met him at the door, his face grave, and pointed to the red, leaping glare in the sky.

"They're coming," he said, hopelessly. "There's nothing we can do to stop them."

James could only nod. He knew that what the man said was true.

"We can't stop them," he agreed, at last. "All we can do is delay them and hope our army isn't far behind."

"Delay them?" Mr. Craig paused for a moment, then turned to look at his house, made from substantial, hand-hewn logs.

"It's not a fort," he said, "and there's not many windows to shoot from, but we might be able to hold them off for a while."

James looked doubtful. "You know what that would mean? Your house would be burned for certain. But if we just continue as we are, firing at them from trees and fences, they might spare it. They might even use it to shelter the officers overnight if they get this far. It's a cold night to sleep outdoors."

Alexander shrugged. "I'm not a soldier. I'll do whatever your sergeant thinks best."

James nodded. "Sergeant Kerr should be here soon. I'll go and scout them out and see if they're likely to come this far tonight. Then we'll decide what's best."

"Then take one of the Indians with you. Take no offence, but they're better at creeping up on the enemy without being caught than any paleface ever was. Black Bird," Alexander raised his arm.

A Mohawk in buckskin, materialized from the deepening shadows.

James told him what he proposed.

Black Bird grinned, showing white teeth. "I'll lead the way. You would give us away for certain." Without another word he turned, silent in his moccasins. James looked at Alexander, grinned, and followed the Mohawk into the dusk.

It was called, sarcastically, the King's Road. It was little more than a rutted track cut through the woods, impassable much of the time because of snow or mud. Just now the ground was hard from an early frost. James had difficulty keeping up with the fleet-footed Indian. But when they drew near the scene – near enough to hear the crackling of the flames – Black Bird put his finger to his lips and drew James into the trees.

"Quiet," he urged. "Tread softly."

Here were roots to stumble over, branches to trip them up, twigs to snap with reports like pistol shots. James followed the silent Indian as best he could, trying to tread lightly in his heavy boots. And when Black Bird stopped suddenly, James almost fell against him.

They had reached the fringe of trees. Before them was the clearing. The house itself was undamaged, but the men were hauling out furniture, pulling down an out-building, dismantling the rail fence, and gathering anything that would burn to keep them warm. Several fires were already lit. Some men were huddled around them. Muskets were stacked neatly nearby. Two supply wagons were there, unhitched. On the far side, on the edge of the forest, four draft horses were tethered.

James caught Black Bird's arm. "They're here for the night," he whispered. "That's plain. That's all we need to know. Let's go."

But Black Bird shook his head. "We want to delay them, don't we? If we stampede those horses now, they won't even begin to look for them till daylight." His dark eyes were dancing with mischief. "Do you agree?"

"How do we do that?"

The Indian surveyed the scene for a moment before answering.

"There's no one guarding the horses yet. If we act quickly we can loosen them, then mount one each." He hesitated. "Do you ride?"

James shook his head ruefully. "We have no horses. Just oxen."

"Then you'd better not try. I'll mount one, give you a

chance to get away, then I'll yell loud enough to spook the horses and the camp as well. Those horses will be back to Prescott before they catch up to them." He looked enquiringly at James. "What do you say?"

James licked his suddenly dry lips. "You lead the way," he said.

The Indian grinned and clapped him on the back. "That's wise. We'll go round...*way* round so they don't hear you creeping through the forest. Follow me."

A few minutes later they approached the camp again from the opposite direction. It looked as if no sentries had been posted yet. A few armed men stood about, but they were more intent on staying within reach of the warmth of the flames than on keeping watch. There didn't seem to be anyone near the horses.

Black Bird paused to reconnoiter.

A line of rope had been stretched between two widely separated trees. The horses were tied to this, each with a tether long enough to permit it to move about and to crop the grass. To free them meant that James and Black Bird would be visible to anyone in the camp who happened to look that way.

Black Bird's hand rested on James' arm. "Have you a sharp knife?"

"Yes."

"Good. Don't waste time trying to untie the ropes. Cut them. Fast. I'll take the two at the far end. Watch for me. When I show myself beyond the far horse, cut these two loose, get out of here as fast as you can and leave the rest to me."

James caught the Indian's hand in a momentary grip. "Good luck," he whispered.

He moved out silently beside the first horse. The animal lifted its head, looking at him enquiringly.

"Shh. Good horse. Take it easy. We're friends." He patted the horse's neck reassuringly, its bulk between him and the camp. He ventured further out, till he knew that he would be seen by anyone looking his way. He felt for the rope he would have to cut and waited, holding his breath.

A movement, at the far end of the line of horses. There was Black Bird, knife in hand. James waited no longer. He slashed at the rope, slashed again. The rope parted.

The surprised animal moved back, feet heavy on the ground, bumping into its neighbor. The second horse reared back, neighing a protest. James grabbed for its tether. The horse jerked its head away, ears flattened, nostrils flaring. It neighed shrilly, reared back, flailing the air with threshing feet.

There were shouts behind him, the sound of running feet. They won't shoot, thought James, for fear of hitting the horses. But they're coming.

He heard Black Bird call out, "Run, James."

But he hadn't cut that second rope yet. It was taut as the horse pulled away. He slashed at it. But at the same moment the horse lunged. He saw a heavy foot coming, tried to dodge. It struck him a glancing blow, sending the knife flying from his hand. He staggered and fell.

He had failed to cut the rope. He had lost his knife. That meant he would have to untie it. Desperately, shutting out the sounds of running feet and shouting voices, he felt for the knot. He found it. But his arm was numb, his fingers useless. Tears of frustration blinded him.

Someone was coming at him, a knife raised high to strike.

He threw up his good arm to defend himself.

The knife came down, slashing the rope.

He saw Black Bird grab the horse's mane and leap onto its back as lightly as dandelion down caught in the breeze.

"Run, James." he yelled. Then his war cry shivered through the night.

James turned, launching himself to his feet. But one of the enemy soldiers was almost onto him, grabbing for him, catching his coat. He wrenched free. But the other came again in a flying tackle. James crashed to the ground.

He twisted, trying to free himself, and found himself looking into his captor's face.

For a brief, eternal moment they stared at each other.

"Jared!"

"James! Oh, God!"

Then Jared looked back over his shoulder. "They're coming." He released his grip. "Go, James. Run."

And James ran into the dark shelter of the forest.

Chapter Twenty-Two

T he British-Canadian army, a mixture of regulars, militia and Indians, caught up with the Americans in the vicinity of John Crysler's farm.

Lieutenant-Colonel Joseph Morrison was not anxious to fight. He was well aware that his force was outnumbered almost ten to one. But if battle was unavoidable, and he was pretty sure that was the case, then he wanted the battle to be fought on terrain where his veterans training could be used to advantage. He found such a site on John Crysler's wheatfields.

A stout rail fence almost the width of the property would provide protection to stall the first attack. To the left was an impassable swamp behind a fringe of trees; to the right, only the King's Highway was between the fence and the river. And in front of the fence was a broad expanse of cultivated land scarred by gullies and one deep ravine through which a stream ran from the swamp to the river. It wasn't flat and open like the Plains of Abraham, but it was the best he could hope to find on short notice.

The American army landed at Cook's Point, beyond the farm, and prepared for battle, determined to rid itself of the pestilential annoyance that had been following and harassing it for days, before moving on to take Montreal.

In John Crysler's stout farm house, which he had taken over as his headquarters, Colonel Morrison spoke quietly to Rachel, Leah and three other women who had been put ashore from a gunboat.

"There will be a battle fought here today," he said. "I don't know how it will turn out. We are heavily outnumbered. But it is our last chance to save Montreal. The fate of our country rests on our shoulders. If we stop the enemy from going any further, we will have preserved the lifeline at least until next spring, and, quite possibly, permanently. I won't contemplate the result should we lose. We can't afford to lose." He hesitated, looking at the set-faced women before him. "You ladies have the most difficult part to play. You won't know the quickening of the pulse, the pounding of the heart, and the rush of excitement that overpowers fear in the moments when battle is joined. You can only wait and listen to the sounds of war, then go out and view the carnage, and do what you can to aid the wounded, friend and foe alike.

"You have no idea what your presence and your touch will mean to men who have been hurt and mutilated. I can only thank you in advance."

* * *

On the morning of November 11, 1813, a cold wind swept across Crysler's fields, bringing with it a cold rain laced with stinging sleet. Both armies waited it out, shivering in greatcoats and huddled by fires that sputtered and died. Then the skies cleared, leaving the field a sea of mud and swollen streams rushing through ravines to the river.

The Americans sent out a scouting party to feel out the enemy. They advanced, keeping close to the fringe of trees that separated the field from the swamp.

Suddenly, from behind every tree, from behind every rock, and out of every hollow, gray-coated men sprang up and poured a volley of musket fire into the advancing army.

James was one of them. As he bit off the end of another cartridge and poured powder into the firing pan with shaking fingers, he saw the surprised foe waver, then fire their guns at random. A second volley drove the Americans back in confusion.

But the Americans were not beaten. They regrouped, and they came on, a tide this time that could not be stopped. It was James and his fellows who fell back before that unyielding surge of blue-coated men. And the Canadian force were well aware that there was a dire threat in that relentless advance. Unless the Americans were stopped, they would encircle the main army behind the fence and attack it from its defenceless rear.

But the Americans were in for a surprise. The red-coated men of the 89th regiment had been trained to know what to do in such a situation. Standing shoulder to shoulder, at a word of command, they moved as one unit, executing a parade ground manoeuvre that brought them around in a solid line. When the Americans broke from the woods, they found themselves facing a red, unbroken wall that poured a thunderous volley into them. They turned and fled.

From then on James scarcely knew what was happening. Both sides brought up artillery that cut swathes through the opposing ranks. Another attempt to encircle the British line – this time along the river bank by dragoons thundering down the King's Highway – was again thwarted in the same way. Terrified, wounded horses plunged and fell, neighing shrilly. Those that could, galloped off with empty saddles.

Of all this James was unaware. He only knew what was going on in his own sector. Separated from the militia, he was swept along by the advancing British veterans who had left their defences and were on the attack. His ears ached from the sound of the irregular, individual American guns and the thunderous reply of British guns firing in unison. He saw men moving like ghosts through the smoke that rolled across the field. He saw men fall, cry out in agony, and die. He saw severed limbs and bloody corpses. He felt the drag of mud on his feet. He plunged through a ravine where icy water chilled him to the thighs. He fired his musket, and there was no time to reload. There was only his bayonet and the stock of his gun to be swung like a club.

Surrounded by red-coated soldiers, he bore down on the American cannons that were spewing death into the British ranks. One of them belched smoke and flames, seemingly directly in front of him. The arm of his coat was torn off at the shoulder by the blast. The man beside him cried out, spun around with flailing arms, and died. The gap torn in the ranks by the blast was filled by more men swarming over the fallen. The gun crew turned and fled.

In the momentary lull, James reloaded his musket and moved like an automaton, all feelings washed away in the slaughter. He looked around dully.

He saw an American soldier kneeling, taking aim at a British officer who was rallying his men with flourished sword. James fired. The American soldier dropped his gun, spun round, clutched his side, and fell.

James stared in mounting horror. In that moment he recognized his victim. Jared!

For one anguished moment James stood there, unaware of a musket ball ripping through his coat, another snatching the cap from his head.

Then he was running, fear pounding in his throat, leaping over the fallen, running, and kneeling beside his friend, staring into the white face, the closed eyes, the ugly red patch spreading over the shirt.

Jared's eyes opened. He smiled weakly. "Hello, James," he whispered. His eyes closed.

But he's not dead, thought James wildly. He can't die.

A heavy gun fired somewhere behind them. Jagged pieces of metal were falling all around them. James flung himself across Jared.

Something struck him on the back of his head. Blood misted his eyes. He lost consciousness.

An hour later, Leah found them.

Chapter Twenty-Three

The battle of Crysler's Farm did not end the war. There were still battles to be won or lost, homes to be burned, and men to be mutilated and die before it all ended in a stalemate.

But it dashed the Americans' hopes of driving a wedge between the Canadas, and ended their hopes of making Canada another state in the Union.

And it brought lasting peace to the valley of the St. Lawrence. The people on both sides of the river began putting their lives back together again.

It was a Friday morning. Blue skies and a warming sun gave promise of approaching spring.

James turned the canoe into land, stepped ashore, and pulled the canoe up behind him. He looked toward the Jacksons' home. There was a plume of smoke rising from the chimney. Otherwise there was no sign of life.

Suddenly his heart was thumping, his face damp with anxiety. He had almost killed Jared. Did they know that? Could they ever forgive him? Would he ever be welcome here again?

Leah. He could hardly believe it when his mother told him what she had done, in an effort to prevent what eventually happened anyway. She must have cared an awful lot. For her brother? Or James? Both, surely? And she had found them – Jared and James – on that field of death, and had nursed them until her father had come and taken her and Jared back home. And James hadn't even known it. By the time he had recovered well enough to know what was going on, she was gone. And he had never even thanked her.

Did they – did she – know it was James' gun that had brought Jared down? Maybe not. Jared probably didn't know it himself. Perhaps they only believed that he had saved Jared's life by shielding his body from the shower of bullets. Then James would be a hero. But *he* knew what had happened. He would have to tell them. Otherwise there would always be that secret between them – an invisible barrier.

Then would Leah forgive him? Even if she did, would her father let her see him? The war was still on. He was still the enemy.

So he stood there, in an agony of indecision, unanswered questions bringing sweat to his brow. He shouldn't have come. Not yet. Not till the war was over, if then. He turned back to the canoe.

The door opened behind him. He stopped, rooted, not daring to look back. Then there was a joyful bark, and suddenly Pilot was jumping all over him, tail wagging furiously. Pilot, at least...

He knelt to pat the dog and fondle its ears. And he heard someone coming softly over the grass behind him. He held his breath.

"Hello, Jamie."

Jamie. Only Leah called him that. And her voice was as gentle and musical as ever. His heart thumped.

He turned. He looked at her and was tongue-tied.

For a moment they stood, looking at each other. And he knew that she still cared, and all he had to do was reach out and take her hand in his. But he didn't.

"Leah," he said, harshly, "I shot Jared. Did you know that?"

She nodded. "I knew, Jamie. You were delirious. You raved all about it, so I know. And I know you saved his life afterward too."

"And Jared? Does he know?"

"Yes. We all know."

"Is he...is he all right?

"Yes, he's fine. He has a scar where they dug a musket ball out of his side, but he has recovered. Fully. He will come out to see you in a few minutes, but he said he would give you and me a little while together first. He wants to thank you."

"Thank me! Even though he knows...I should thank

him. He let me go once, when he could have held onto me and màde me a prisoner. If he had, none of this would have happened. Did you know about that too?"

"Oh yes. He told us. We know everything, Jamie."

"We? Your father too?"

"Even father. He knows you were just doing your duty when you...when you shot Jared. And more than your duty when you shielded him. Even to him, you are no longer an enemy."

"I'm not? Then, Leah, there's nothing between us anymore?"

"Nothing, Jamie. Except..." She looked down. "...except a foot or two of empty space."

"Oh." He looked into her dark, star-lit eyes. "Oh. Leah..."

And there was nothing at all between them any more.

Glossary

Bateau   A lightweight, flat-bottomed boat.

Blue-coat   A general term for American soldiers,
                    although not all regiments wore blue.

Breastwork   A low wall put up quickly as a defence
                    in battle.

Byre   A cow barn, stable.

Canister   A cylinder of shot that explodes
                    on impact.

Carronade   A short, light cannon with a large bore
                    used at close range.

Cutter   A boat or small vessel that can cut
                    swiftly through the water.

Epaulette   A shoulder ornament of military and
                    naval officers. Also spelled epaulet.

Fusillade   A simultaneous or rapid and continuous
                    discharge of many firearms.

Grapeshot   A cluster of small iron balls or jagged bits of metal fired from a cannon.

Gunboat   A small, armed ship of shallow draft used to patrol rivers.

Gunwale   The upper edge of the side of a ship (or gunnel) or boat.

Mortar   A short-barreled cannon for firing shells at high angles.

Militia   An army of civilians called out in time of emergency.

Musket   A smooth-bore, long-barreled firearm fired from the shoulder.

NCO   Noncommissioned officer.

Oarlock   A device for holding an oar in place.

Painter   A rope attached to the bow of a boat for mooring.

Palisade   A row of large, pointed stakes set close together to form a fence.

Pounder   A gun carrying a shell of a specific number of pounds.

Redcoat   A general term for British soldiers, although not all regiments wore red.

Salvo   The simultaneous firing of a number
                of guns.

Settle   A long seat or bench with a high back.

Shako   A tall, stiff, cylindrical military hat.

Sweep   A long oar.

Thwart   A rower's seat extending across
                the boat.

Tinderbox   A metal box for holding flammable
                material; flint and steel for starting
                a fire.

Whaler   A large, long rowboat pointed at
                both ends.

To learn more about the War of 1812:

The Invasion of Canada by Pierre Berton,
McClelland & Stewart
ISBN 0-7710-1235-7 copyright 1980

Flames Across the Border by Pierre Berton,
McClelland & Stewart
ISBN 0-7710-1244-6 copyright 1981

Robert Sutherland is the author of a number of mystery and historical novels for juvenile and young adult readers, including *Mystery at Black Rock Island*, *The Loon Lake Murders*, *Son of the Hounds*, *The Fugitive*, *The Ghost of Ramshaw Castle*, *Suddenly a Spy*, *Death Island*, and *The Secret of Devil Lake*. His work has been nominated for the *Silver Birch Award*, the *Arthur Ellis Award for Best Juvenile Novel*, the *Geoffrey Bilson Historical Fiction Award*, and the *Canadian Library Association Book of the Year*. He lives near Kingston, Ontario, with his family.